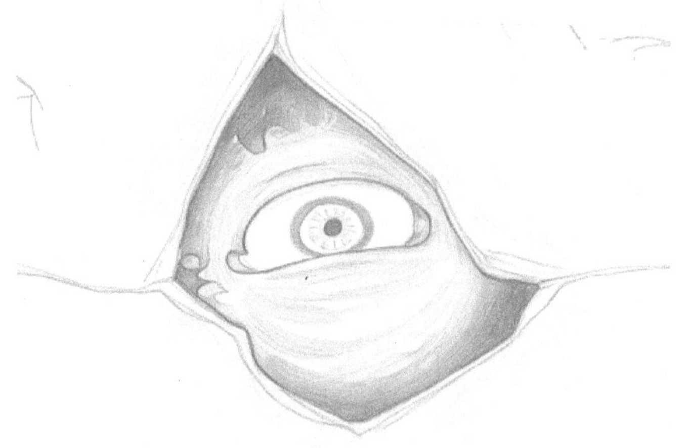

LOSING AIR

DARK AND STRANGE TALES

LOSING AIR

DARK AND STRANGE TALES

AVA CHRISTINA

Pen & Sword Press
Tri-Cities, WA

This is a work of fiction. All characters and events in this work are either products of the author's imagination or are used fictitiously.

LOSING AIR: DARK AND STRANGE TALES

Cover art by Olivia Rojas
Cover design by Ava Christina
Cover layout by L. Saige Johnson
Author photo by Angela Garcia-Moog

Published by Pen & Sword Press

www.penandsword.blog

ISBN 979-8-218-91284-0 (paperback)
ISBN 979-8-218-91285-7 (ebook)

First Edition

For anyone who finds joy in the dark.

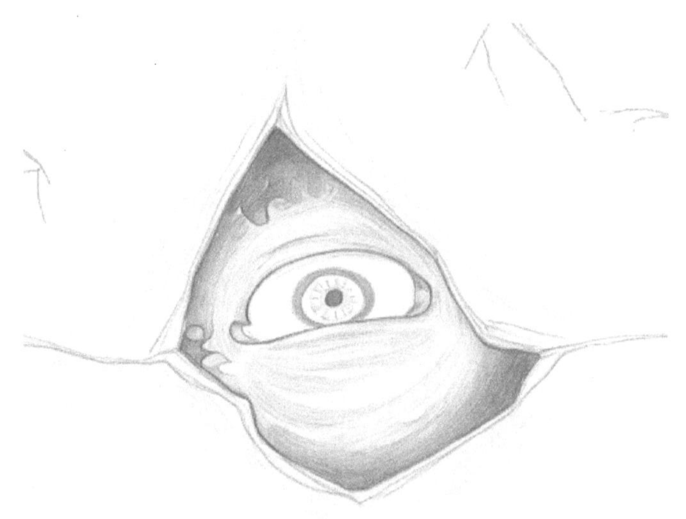

LOSING AIR

DARK AND STRANGE TALES

CONTENTS

SOPHIE

This story is very special to me as it was my very first to be published. During this time I was reading a lot of grief horror, such as Gus Moreno's This Thing Between Us *and Gerardo Sámano Córdova's* Monstrilio, *so the grief angle really kind of wrote itself.*
This story was originally published in the September 2025 issue of Tumbleweird.

Two weeks after Ben Wright's wife and daughter died, he returned to the cemetery.

He drove his safety-conscious Corolla, the last payment made only two months earlier, up the hill. The verges were lined with manicured grass, turning brown and soon to be buried under snow. He had the windows down, and the late October wind fought desperately against the car's heating system.

Ben didn't feel the cold — he was drunk.

The next day, Ben wouldn't remember clicking off his headlights before turning into Rose Hill Memorial Gardens. He parked, alone in the lot at two in the morning, and popped the trunk, the click echoing across the dark pavement. Ben retrieved the bouquet of flowers inside. He wouldn't remember that either.

Anyone seeing the shambling form of Ben Wright stumbling across the wet leaves may have imagined zombies, or barrowmen, or serial killers with broken minds, had there been any mourners there at that late hour. But no one was around to witness his foot go into a gopher hole, sending him sprawling. He rolled instinctively, stood up, and continued — didn't even stop to dust the dirt and leaves off his shoulder.

He wandered through the gardens, stopping occasionally to read a grave marker, his final destination two headstones, side by side, unmarked by weather and time. The headstones were a formality — the coffins buried beneath them were empty, save for a yellow sundress in one and a stuffed toy dog in the smaller.

Ben bent to one knee, his jeans soaking through on the damp ground. A leaf was stuck to the headstone on the right and he angrily plucked it away. A low, awful sound emanated from his throat. Ben wasn't aware of it. His arm felt suddenly numb and he dropped the flowers. He stared at the headstones. Tears streamed silently down his face.

"Daddyshere," he slurred, the words mushy in his mouth, like the applesauce he used to feed his daughter in her stained highchair.

The breeze strengthened, howling gusts of biting cold buffeting his bare face and hands, shaking off the last stubborn leaves from the neat rows of trees planted throughout the graveyard.

Ben heard a rustle in the fallen leaves behind him. His reflexes dulled by drink, he spun slowly — a toy dancer in a music box. His vision blurred, flickered in and out, his consciousness darkening.

He could barely make out a small shape in the bushes.

As he fell into blackness, one word came through: "...Daddy?"

Ben would remember none of this. By the next morning, the only remainder of the night before was raw, sharp emotion — the pain of his grief and loss a spearhead in his ribs.

Following the death of Ben Wright's wife and daughter, his brother, Paul, came to stay with him.

The tragedy had torn through the entire family. That little girl was the best thing that had ever happened to them. She was always smiling, even through her tears when she scraped a knee or hit her head on the playground. At the double memorial, Ben and Paul's mother had broken out in hysterical, haunting wails as their sister sang "Somewhere Over the Rainbow". She'd been drunk. Hell, most of them had been drunk.

Pain like that had to be dulled with something.

The moment he had received the call, Paul told his supervisor he would be out for bereavement, and set up camp at Ben's house. It felt empty and too quiet. He slept on the couch.

He'd been there for three days — cooking meals, taking out trash, doing dishes, and washing the backed-up laundry — before his brother finally began speaking, in little leaks, like a faucet left dripping.

They were sitting on the couch, pretending to watch the evening news, beers warming in their hands.

"She was leaving," said Ben.

"What?"

"We fought. It was one of those fights where nothing's really the matter, you just both need a break and don't know it. You know?"

Paul said he did, even though he was a bachelor. He didn't know squat about relationships.

An hour later, the Wheel of Fortune spinning for the umpteenth time, Ben said, "It's my fault."

Paul's response was a reflex: "No, it's not."

Ben stared at the puzzle slowly filling in on the screen.

"She said she was going to Judith's. To get away from me. She was so mad. I was, too."

Paul didn't know what to say.

Another hour passed. The washer beeped. "I better rotate the laundry," Paul said.

"I almost stopped her. I knew she'd stay if I begged. But I was just so mad at her." Ben drank the last sip of his beer.

"It's not your fault," Paul repeated. "If you want to blame somebody, blame the truck driver that pulled out in front of her."

Ben didn't look away from the TV. "She wouldn't have been out there, out there with her in the back seat, if I had swallowed my pride."

Later, Paul lugged a basket of fresh laundry into Ben's bedroom. He glanced at the door and listened. Hearing no sound of Ben moving from the couch, he opened the closet and reached to the top shelf. The Smith & Wesson Model 12 was exactly where he expected to find it. When he took the trash out before bed, Paul stopped by his car and tucked the gun under the driver's seat.

After a week of Paul sleeping on his couch, Ben told his brother he thought he would be okay on his own.

"I appreciate you being here. I'm alright now. I know it was rough at the beginning, but the shock's passed. Thanks for taking care of things around here," Ben said, and pulled him in for what passed for a hug between men — a quick, simultaneous smack on the back.

"Call me anytime, bud. I'm here," Paul said.

"Sure. Yeah. I'll keep you posted."

Paul didn't hear from Ben for a week.

Ben woke slowly, like rising out of deep water. His head was heavy and spinning. How much did I drink?

"Daddy!"

Sophie appeared in the open bedroom doorway. She was wearing her Paw Patrol pajamas.

Oh thank God! It was only a nightmare! But it felt so real?! "Yes, Honey-bun?"

"I'm hungry," Sophie whined.

Ben rubbed his face with his hand. It was dirty. He didn't notice. "Sorry, Daddy didn't mean to sleep in."

"Can we make pancakes?" she asked, bouncing on her toes.

Ben smiled, feeling like a rich man. "Alright, but don't tell Mommy. She says I put in too much sugar." He swung his legs over the side of the bed and stuck his feet into his slippers. "She must be at work already."

"Mommy's gone," confirmed Sophie.

Ben passed her in the doorway, ruffling her thin, blonde hair and smiling down at her. "If that's the case, I think I'll add chocolate chips this time."

Paul paced his tiny living room. "Damn it, Ben, answer the fucking phone!"

Is he angry with me? He might have noticed his gun was gone. But Paul couldn't regret getting that out of the house. Grief could warp people's minds and he didn't want to lose a brother, too.

Paul knew Ben needed space to grieve, but he had hoped to hear something from him at least once a day — a text, a call, any proof of life. This total silence was distressing.

He typed out a text and hit send: Just checking in. You okay?

The message was delivered and opened, but no response came.

"Damn it, Ben," Paul spat again, and continued to pace.

"Do you want a drink, Honey-bun?" Ben called from the kitchen while he stirred the batter.

"Yes please, Daddy!" Sophie called back from where she sat in front of the TV, watching cartoons and bouncing her heels against the couch.

"What do you want?"

"Hmm. Apple juice!"

Ben paused, raising an eyebrow. He looked at her over the breakfast bar, confused. "I thought you hated apple juice."

Sophie's feet went still and her back stiffened. It was a few moments before she resumed her carefree swinging.

"I like it again," she said lightly.

Ben almost responded, *You've never liked it*, but stopped himself. The whims of children were unpredictable, their tastes constantly changing.

"Okay, Hon. Just don't spill any on the couch or Mommy will have my hide."

Paul called his mother. He hadn't stopped pacing all morning.

"You're sure he's reading your texts?" she asked.

"I mean, yeah, I can see that he's read them."

"I think you should go check on him."

"I guess so," Paul said. "I'm sure he's fine, I just don't get why he can't send back a simple I'm okay, you know? He must know we'd be worried."

"Get over there and let me know how it goes."

"Okay, Mom. I love you."

"I love you too, Paulie."

"Honey-bun?"

"Yes, Daddy?"

"Have you seen Daddy's phone anywhere?"

Ben lifted the couch cushions while Sophie, at the kitchen table, ate her pancakes with surprising dexterity.

"No, Daddy." Sophie stuck a huge forkful of pancake in her small mouth.

"Damn," Ben swore. Quietly, so she didn't hear him. "Could've sworn I just had it."

The little girl at the table swung her feet and watched her daddy search the living room while she chewed and swallowed bite after bite of syrupy goodness. In the waistband of her pajama pants, a hard, black rectangle vibrated against her skin.

Arriving at Ben's house, Paul's stomach roiled. He was imagining worst-case scenarios — *Ben bought another gun and did not tell me. Ben swallowed the entire bottle of Ibuprofen in the bathroom cabinet. Ben ran off, in the middle of a breakdown, and abandoned everyone.*

But his car was still there, so that last one could probably be ruled out. There was an empty space next to it where Ben's wife's car would never be parked again. It was totalled in the accident — crushed to the size of a port-o-potty by the semi-truck.

Paul threw open his car door and stepped onto the asphalt. As he started towards the house, he caught a flicker of movement behind the curtains. Relief flooded through him, immediately replaced by irritation.

He's alive! He could answer a text!

Paul stomped up the walk and rang the doorbell.

Sophie sat in the bath, buried deep in pink bubbles. Her bath toys floated around her. The tiny child's sharp gaze was unflinchingly glued to the bathroom door, watching her daddy through the few inches he had left it open.

Ben moved around Sophie's bedroom, collecting clean clothes to warm in the dryer. He pulled a pink T-shirt with flowers off a small hanger in her closet and turned to lay it on her bed.

"What the hell?" Ben murmured.

Her pink Rainbow High comforter was bunched at the end of the small bed, revealing the matching sheets, covered in dirt and wet leaves. Ben stared at the bed for a long time, uncomprehending. *Did Sophie go outside before she woke me?*

He stripped the bed and brought the comforter and sheets to the laundry room. He put Sophie's clothes for the day into the dryer, then stuffed the bed dressings into the washer and turned it on.

When he returned to the bathroom, Sophie was playing with her boat.

"Hey, Honey?"

"Yes, Daddy?"

He sat on the closed toilet.

"Did you play outside this morning, before you woke me?" he asked gently, not wanting to put her on the defensive.

Sophie splashed the bathwater with her boat, laughing. "No, Daddy."

"How'd you get all that dirt and leaves in your bed then?"

Sophie let the boat go still on the water. When she looked at him, Ben was startled by the calculation in her eyes. Gone was the open, curious, innocent expression of his four-year-old. She didn't smile. Just held his eyes with a much-too-intelligent gaze.

Ben, unnerved, pulled away, backing toward the bathroom door.

"Sophie?" His voice shook.

The doorbell rang.

Paul texted his mother: *At his place now. I'll let you know.*

He tried calling Ben's phone one more time, but there was no answer. Paul rang the doorbell again, his heart picking up speed.

I'm gonna give him a thrashing for freaking me out like this.

Ben jumped at the sound of the doorbell. He didn't know what to do about his suddenly terrifying four-year-old, so he tried to act normal.

"I'll be right back," he said to Sophie.

He hurried to the laundry room. As he retrieved the warm clothes and towel from the dryer, he had a creepy feeling he was being watched.

The hell is going on?

He went towards the bathroom, where his little girl waited for him, but he was afraid. He didn't want to look in her eyes again and see that uncanny intelligence.

He and his wife had always known Sophie was a bright child, but what he'd seen in her face was a wisdom far beyond her years. When she'd caught his gaze, it was like she saw straight through him, as if his body was a sheet, and she'd shone a light behind it, casting the shadow of all his private thoughts against the wall.

I know about the pack of cigarettes taped under the kitchen counter, her eyes had told him. *I know about the adult videos you watch when mom takes me out and leaves you alone. I know about the emotional affair you had three years ago with that coworker.*

Ben's legs were weak as he forced himself to walk into the room, warm fabric crumpled in his arms.

Sophie was playing in the bathtub with her toys, just like any normal child. *What was I freaking out about? That's my little girl right there!* He smiled at her, and she smiled back, her short baby teeth poking out of pink gums. He'd completely forgotten about the dirt and leaves in her bed.

"Alright, Honey-bun, time to get out."

He expected her to protest, but she rose from the water, using her hands to brush off the bubbles stuck to her skin. He lifted her out of the tub and held up her warm, pink towel. She stepped into it with no fuss and he wrapped it around her small, damp body.

"Can you get dry and dressed by yourself, Honey-bun? Someone's at the door."

As if to enforce his point, the doorbell rang a second time.

Sophie began drying herself. "Yes, Daddy."

He set the clothes on the lid of the toilet and left the bathroom, again leaving the door slightly open.

Sophie dropped the towel to the floor. She kept her eyes on the door as she reached back with both hands and felt along her spine.

Her fingers found the jagged line, the almost invisible depression where the skin joined, and she slipped inside, her arms bending at impossible angles. They seemed to grow longer out of the sockets where they met her narrow shoulders.

Sophie pulled the vibrating cell phone out of her body. A man who looked like a longer, thinner version of her daddy smiled at her from the screen. The text above him read 'Paul'.

She felt a shock of irritation. Her eyes blackened for a split second, then returned to their normal baby blue.

She returned the phone to the wet crevice in her back. The tissue squelched around it, sucking the device into her body, and the skin closed, the seam undetectable to anyone who didn't know it was there.

Sophie heard her daddy arrive at the front door and dressed as fast as she could.

Ben checked his face in the entryway mirror and wiped a bit of leftover chocolate from his lip, smoothed down some stray hairs, and deemed himself presentable.

Taking a deep breath, he threw the deadbolt and opened the front door.

"Oh, hey Paul."

Paul's brother looked fine. Freshly shaved, dressed in clean clothes, and rested. Not at all like a man whose entire family died two weeks ago.

Paul gaped at Ben, unable to speak. *What is happening?*

"What's up, bro?" said Ben, when he didn't respond.

"Are— Is everything alright, Ben?"

Ben raised his eyebrows. "Yeah? Why wouldn't it be? Are you alright?"

"I— it's just— You weren't answering your phone. You freaked me out. Mom, too."

Ben stretched and scratched his chest. "Ah, yeah, I can't find my phone. Haven't seen it all day. Might've lost it while I was out last night. Drank way too much."

"You haven't answered my calls or texts for almost a week, Ben." Paul studied his brother, his eyes narrowing. Something is wrong.

Ben furrowed his eyebrows. "Really? I don't remember getting anything from you since we went to LaRocca's."

That was two and a half weeks ago! When they'd gotten together for dinner at LaRocca's, they'd had a good time together. Ben's wife and daughter were killed on the highway four days later.

Paul's heart was pounding. *Can Ben hear it?* "What are you talking about, Ben? Is this some fucking joke or something?"

"Is what a joke? No, I haven't gotten anything from you since we went to dinner. Are you sure your phone is working?" Ben seemed genuinely confused.

What. Is. Happening?

"Uncle Paul?" A small, high voice rang from inside the house.

Paul felt like he had been punched in the gut. His stomach clenched and when he tried to breathe, he couldn't get any air. The skin on his scalp was hot and prickling — like molten wax dripping from his crown, down around his ears.

"What the fuck?" Paul's throat was so tight he could barely force the words out.

Ben ignored him. "Hey Honey-bun! Wanna say 'hi' to Uncle Paul?"

"Yeah!"

Sophie appeared from behind Ben and slipped her little hand into her father's.

That's not possible. She's dead! She's been dead for two weeks. I saw the car — an unidentifiable ball of twisted metal! It's not possible! Paul's throat closed, as if filled with wool, and he thought he would choke.

"Hi, Uncle Paul," Sophie chirped.

Paul's desire for a wife and children had dampened the moment he held Sophie for the first time. He was content watching her grow into a small person — teaching her new words, helping her work through challenges, and showing her his favorite childhood TV shows. He-Man and Thundercats were particular favorites when he'd streamed them for her last Christmas. Her death had devastated him.

How is this possible?!

The entryway mirror behind Ben caught Paul's eye and he glanced at it, instantly recoiling — beside the reflections of his face and his brother's back was a creature, horribly brown and rotten. Clumps of knotted black hair clung to the skull, worms wriggling through them; scraps of skin dangled off the ochre bones; and wet leaves clung to scraps of clothing hanging from the shoulders, no longer serving any purpose.

When he looked back, horrified, the child in front of him looked like his niece. No hint of rot or decay clung to her. She hung onto his brother, her tiny hand enveloped by his huge one. She was wearing the same pink T-shirt he'd cleaned vomit off of, after she ate too much candy last Halloween. Paul peered closer at the little girl's face. Her eyes narrowed and her mouth widened into a sly grin.

Whatever this thing is, it's not Sophie! He turned to run. *Gotta get away! Fuck fuck fuck*!

The thing that looked like Sophie screeched — hair-raising, inhuman.

Paul had only taken one step when something impossibly heavy landed on his back and yanked him into the house.

Ben couldn't comprehend what was going on — it happened so fast. He saw Sophie leap onto his brother's shoulders in a twisted approximation of a piggy-back ride. Ben pulled back hard, banging his head on the wall behind him.

"Sophie!" His ears were ringing and he shook his head to clear the noise. *She's four years old! A baby!*

Still sucks her thumb and calls pajamas 'jammies'! What is she doing?!

Paul lurched into the living room. Sophie clung to his shoulders, her arms lengthening and wrapping around his throat, compressing his windpipe. Ben could see him trying to scream. The only sound that came out was a whispered rasp. He looked directly at Ben, his eyes bulging and terrified.

Ben stood frozen, gaping — his brain malfunctioning. The front door hung open like a hungry mouth. Outside, it was afternoon and the weather was calm. A playful October breeze pushed back the stagnant, hot air inside the house and rays of sunlight trailed in, warming Ben's skin. He didn't notice.

Paul heaved, throwing himself against the cabinet in the living room, trying to dislodge Sophie from his back. The cabinet doors shattered, the crash echoing through the house. She did not let go, even though several large, jagged pieces of glass impaled her.

Where's the blood? Ben thought distantly. He couldn't move.

Sophie tightened her hold and Paul slowly stopped fighting, like a toy running out of batteries. He scrabbled at those unearthly, too-long arms, trying to pry them from his neck, his fingernails raking strips of bloodless skin. As he ran out of breath, he lost his grip, staggered; his feet tangled and he hit the carpet, face first, twitching.

Now there was blood. It stained the floor, draining from Paul's body where it had been shredded by broken glass. Sophie clung to him like a tick on a dog.

Ben, released from whatever force had been holding him, closed the front door.

Paul's phone, tucked in his jeans pocket where he couldn't reach it, was vibrating. A text from his mother, probably. He knew she was worried and waiting to hear from him.

The Sophie-thing's arms tightened around his throat. The feel of the rotting, putrid body beneath the illusion of her skin made him want to scream, but he could only open his mouth. No sound came out. He reached a bleeding hand out to his brother, his fingers scrabbling at the floor. *Help me!*

Ben stood at the front door, silent, his eyes blank, unresponsive.

Paul kept his eyes on his brother's until his vision went black.

Ben felt like he was coming out of a fog. He could see Paul slumped on the carpet, his slack face digging into twinkling shards of glass, which spread across the living room floor like demented snowflakes.

"Sophie?" Ben's voice strengthened. "What—what are you doing?"

Sophie looked up at him, her hair falling back from her cherubic face, blue eyes wide and innocent. A shard of glass four inches long jutted from her neck, another from her forehead. Sophie wrapped her tiny fingers around the shard in her neck and yanked it out. The skin was torn, but there was no blood.

Ben remembered when he was a kid and his cousin left her Barbie dolls out and his German Shepherd puppy, Huey, chewed on their soft heads — flesh-coloured plastic left all jagged-edged from his developing teeth. That's what Sophie's flesh looked like as she pulled shards of glass out of it with her bare hands.

Ben vomited chocolate pancakes onto the carpet and his vision blurred.

"You're not Sophie!" he gasped.

The Sophie-thing ignored him. She climbed over Paul's body, holding a shard tightly in her right hand, and squatted next to his head. When she lifted Paul's head by the hair and plunged the shard into the soft meat of his throat, Ben thumped to the floor in a faint.

Sophie extracted Paul's vibrating phone from his pocket. She pressed the button on the side and swiped up on the screen with too much dexterity for a four-year-old.

A text message from 'Ma' appeared: *I'm coming over there unless you answer me right now.*

Sophie scanned the message with a smile — the real Sophie wouldn't have been able to read it — then slipped the phone into the slit in her back to join her daddy's.

Sophie — much too strong for a four-year-old — lifted her daddy onto the couch and placed a pillow beneath his head. She kissed his temple, then scuttled to the easy chair to wait. She ignored Paul's lifeless body lying twisted a few feet away.

Ben rose again from blackness. His head pounded. His stomach ached. His mouth was dry and sour.

He groaned. *Am I hungover? What's that smell?*

His eyes came into focus and he saw what sat in the easy chair opposite him — a rotting, stinking being, draped with necrotic skin, upright and still. It watched him with 'eyes' that were merely black holes of shadow in a fleshless skull.

He flinched and bolted upright on the couch with a yell.

He blinked, looked again. The monster was gone. It was just Sophie, in her pink T-shirt, bloodless flaps of skin hanging from her bones. His Sophie, who called pajamas 'jammies' and—

Ben saw two caskets, one normal-sized and one child-sized. He saw his mother and Paul and his sister and cousins and uncles standing around two freshly-dug graves. His sister's voice, singing "... *blue birds flyyyy*..." rose over his mother's, wailing —

He saw the car, crushed to the size of a phone booth. He heard a voice telling him they hadn't suffered; it was instantaneous—

Ben's body froze, his mind screaming: It wasn't a dream.

He watched the Sophie-thing like a rabbit being stalked by a fox. It sat quietly, flayed skin hanging from its forehead and neck like raw chicken.

"What are you?" he croaked.

The Sophie-thing gazed at him with Sophie's blue eyes.

"I heard your soul cry out," it said. It spoke with Sophie's voice, but devoid of emotion. "You were so sad. Your soul was screaming for your Sophie. I felt it there, in the graveyard. Her body wasn't in the casket, of course. You knew that. She was nothing but a spray of blood."

"Stop!" Ben's head was spinning. *Don't let me pass out again!*

"I can be your Sophie. I brought her back to you. This is her skin. Do you like it?" The jagged flaps of skin hanging from its neck bounced as it spoke.

"You don't need your wife. I could feel that. Once you had Sophie, once you had me, she was unnecessary. All your love was for me."

"Please stop! What do you want?" Ben was crying now, uncontrollably — gasping for air, snot pouring from his nose.

"For us to be together. I'll be your Sophie. We don't need anyone else. It'll be just us. Uncle Paul didn't understand. He was just going to get in the way."

Ben looked at his brother, as if seeing him for the first time. Paul's throat was ripped open. A dark puddle, almost black, spread out from it, ruining the plush, cream carpet his wife had installed five years before. *I told her that color would stain.*

Ben shook his head, trying to clear his thoughts. *No, no, no. This can't be happening.*

"It's okay, Daddy. He didn't want us to be together. I had to get rid of him. For us."

As he watched, its eyes turned black as if filling with ink. Its next words emanated with a lower, toneless pitch.

"I am Sophie. My mommy died in a car crash but I survived. It's you and me now, just us forever. I call pajamas 'jammies' and I suck my thumb and I wear Goodnites to bed, but only the ones with the Disney princesses on them. Go put Uncle Paul in the bathtub, Daddy."

That last word pitched up again, and it was his little girl talking. Ben felt his panic receding. Wait—

On some level, he was alarmed, aware that he was being controlled, hypnotized. But as he fell further, all fear drained from him.

He blinked. His baby — his little girl, his Sophie — sat on the easy chair, swinging her legs and smiling. Her skin was pink, unblemished. Her eyes shone as blue as the October sky he could see outside the window.

"Okay, Honey-bun," he said, standing and reaching to ruffle her wispy, blonde hair.

He bent down and grabbed his brother's body by the ankles.

The doorbell rang.

Sophie dropped her doll and ran to the living room.

"I'll get it!" she called to Ben, who was washing the breakfast dishes.

"Okay, Honey-bun," he said, still smiling. He loved spending quality time with his daughter.

Sophie threw the deadbolt and whipped the door open, a hungry grin breaking across her angelic face.

"Hi, Grandma!"

Special thanks to Lari, whose editing skills turned a dull rock into a shining gem.

CHOKE

This was originally written for Pen & Sword as a flash piece for fun. It's got a bit of a sci-fi tinge to it, and hopefully it'll gross you out a bit too. It's the first of two pieces in this collection that are about combat trauma, an issue often ignored in our soldiers that return home after seeing horrors we can't imagine.

I blinked, and the ground beneath me seemed to shudder, almost throwing me off my feet.

I managed to steady myself as the scene around me began to take form. I figured this had to be the final test, or at least close to it. Dr. Jenks had promised nothing in here could actually hurt me, that it was all a product of the simulation being plugged into my head.

But the bleeding slash in my left tricep suggested otherwise. It stung like hell.

The pixels of the simulation finished loading, and I looked out upon a…

Wait, really?

A house. At night. The windows were broken and boarded over, weeds grew thick in the yard. The front door gaped halfway open, crooked on broken hinges. The roof on one side was caved in, moonlight streaming in through the splintered opening.

"Jenks," I said, eyebrows raised. "Did you load the wrong simulation? This is a… a fuckin' haunted house."

Jenks's voice came down on me from nowhere and everywhere, his words projected into my mind from his computer hookup. "This was not an error, Leon."

I blew out a short laugh. "Jenks, I thought we were testing the injection. Superhuman reflexes, and all that?"

"That's right, Leon," the doctor said patiently. "But increased reflexes and a heightened combat ability aren't the only valued attributes of our potential supersoldier. You also need to be able to face *fear* and overpower it."

"You might want to change your simulation then. I'm not afraid of ghosts."

"What makes you think ghosts are my test for you?"

I had no response to that, and Dr. Jenks spoke no more. I could almost feel him watching me on his screens, waiting for me to start moving.

I shrugged. If he wanted to waste time on something goofy like this, it wasn't my concern. I was just his lab rat.

The rotting porch steps creaked as I climbed them, my army-issue combat boots *thunking* down loudly in the quiet echo of the empty night. My KA-BAR rested assuredly on my belt, the only weapon I had been allowed for these tests. The goal was to create a soldier that would require the barest of resources to inflict the most damage.

So far, I had demolished everything set in my path. A haunted house was a joke. During my deployment, I'd seen kids blown up in the streets in Afghanistan, seen starving toddlers gnawing on dismembered limbs for sustenance.

Nothing scared you after seeing things like that.

I passed through the frame of the front door and stepped inside the house.

I looked around, inspecting the bleak interior. It was a very detailed simulation, and it had covered every sense. Well, except taste. But I wasn't about to try licking anything in here.

The bottom floor of the house was all one room, mold-covered couches and shattered wooden tables scattered across the floor. A woven rug stained with chunky blood lay gathering dust in the center of the room. In fact, everything was coated in dust. I sneezed despite myself.

He really thought of everything, I marveled. The previous tests had been good simulations, but they hadn't contained this level of detail.

I suddenly realized I could *smell* the reek of this place.

It was a sickly sweet stench, and I recognized it at once. The rich, cloying stench of rotting bodies. I knew it well.

It brought me back in my memories for just a moment. The compound we'd sent nerve gas into three days before. We'd had to wait until the area was safe, since there was a supply order mix-up and we didn't have any masks. Three days those people had been dead in there, rotting in the heat of the desert climate. By the time we swept through, looking for guns, information, communications, they were bloated and various shades of green, purple, or blue. The air was full of their dying bowel excretions, the smell of their sweet rot. Many of them still had their eyes open, and glassy though they were, I felt they tracked my movements through the rooms like the goddamned Mona Lisa.

The smell in this simulation, in Jenks's stupid haunted house, was the *exact* same smell. Like he'd plucked it out of my memories and dropped it in his little funhouse.

The memories turned my skin cold and clammy. I felt my heart speed up, even faster than its 200bpm it'd been pumping since the injection. There was a weird sensation that was like my stomach dropping down to the floor, like when a plane first leaves the ground.

"Jenks," I called out, straining to keep my voice light and free of tremors. "This is ridiculous. Let's do a real test now. Give me another tank to disable or something."

Jenks didn't respond. That bastard.

"You really want to waste all this money on some stupid kiddie—"

I stopped as the words died in my mouth.

One of the moldy couches about ten feet to my left seemed to shudder and breathe, like the cushions were coming to life. It was dark, the only light was the moonlight streaming in through the destroyed windows. It took me a moment to understand what I was seeing.

Lifting itself from the couch was a girl. *The* girl. The one I'd found in the women's room in that compound we gassed.

She'd been curled into a ball. Her sweet, dead stench had filled the room, clinging to the white linoleum. She couldn't have been more than twenty, and she wore pumps and a pencil skirt.

Just some secretary or assistant, she'd been. Just at work, like every other day. She might not have even known she worked for terrorists. She'd been fixing her makeup in the bathroom one minute, then gassed to death the next.

When I had nightmares of that sweep, it wasn't the rotting terrorists that followed me, asked me why I'd killed them, even though I hadn't been the one to set the gas.

It was that girl. Just a secretary.

And here she was, twenty years later, still dead and bloated when she should've been only dusty bones. She peeled herself off the moldy couch and lifted her head, a filthy hijab stained with old vomit holding her hair in its embrace.

This can't be part of the simulation, I thought. *Jenks never heard about the secretary in the bathroom. There's no possible way he'd know about her.*

She was real. A real ghost. Not a simulation.

I choked on the air in my lungs, stumbling backward. I reached for the door, but just as the old doorknob was in my reach, it swung closed on its own with a resounding *boom*, the crooked hinges suddenly straight.

I turned back to the girl. She was on her feet now, and her glassy eyes were trained directly on me.

Then tears rolled down her rotting green cheek, the craters of flesh eaten away catching the salty liquid as it rolled into them.

"*Why did you kill me, Leon*?" she rasped, her voice thick with the fluid of her rotting insides.

I stood frozen, helpless, paralyzed. I could barely respond.

"I'm sorry," I whispered.

Then she was standing before me. My eyes were pulled to hers, the fuzzy haze that had fallen over her irises, obscuring their chocolatey brown hue, boring into my own eyes, which were stinging with the tears of utter terror.

"*I choked on your poison*," she said, her voice bubbling up through her throat as if from underwater. "*Now you will choke.*"

And then her hands were on my throat, and I could feel the wet, sticky skin melting from her decaying fingers as she choked me, and I only stood there, completely immobile. First there was pressure in my lungs, then I began to panic. Pain took over, and I felt something in my throat *snap* under the unearthly pressure of her horrible fingers. Her head twitched to one side and her rotting hijab came unwrapped, falling to the floor, exposing a nest of dense black hair that crawled with a lively nest of maggots. Some fell, catching in the long tresses of her newly freed hair.

My stomach turned itself inside out, and I would've vomited if my throat wasn't being crushed shut by those dead hands.

"*Choke*," she rasped, and the breath that came from her mouth, so close to me now, smelled like every graveyard in the world combined together. My eyes watered and more vomit climbed its way up my throat, only to be stopped by her vice-grip hands, like a kink in a hose.

Then my air truly ran out, and I was gone.

I didn't notice the state Leon was in at first.

I'd been too busy pounding my fists on my keyboard. My visual feed had gone black as soon as Leon entered my haunted house. I knew smashing another keyboard to pieces wouldn't bring the display back, but I was enraged. Leon was the first to test this new simulation, and now I had been blinded for some reason.

Eventually, the smell caught my attention. It was coming from Leon, still seated in the testing chair. Green and orange vomit leaked slowly from the corners of his mouth. His face was blue, as if he'd been choking on it, but he wasn't moving.

"Leon!" I shouted, then pressed the intercom button on my desk phone. "This is Dr. Jenks. I need medical in the sim lab, *now*!" I didn't wait for a response. I jumped up from my chair, knocking it loudly to the floor in my haste to get to Leon.

I quickly unstrapped the harness that held him in place, ripping the sim diodes from his skull. His body sagged as it lost the support of the harness, and I wrapped my arms around him, taking his weight onto me.

I lowered him out of the chair and down to the lab floor, where I laid him on his side, like one was supposed to do to seizing patients so they didn't choke on their vomit. But Leon wasn't seizing. He was still.

"Leon?" I whispered in fear and horror. With a shaking hand, I lifted two fingers and placed them on his neck, feeling for a pulse.

I felt nothing.

But I saw something. Under my fingers. Blue and purple blotches. They lined his neck, and I could clearly make out the shapes of fingers.

For those who didn't come home the same

KOKOPELLI

I was born in Tucson, Arizona, and while I spent most of my childhood in the Tri-Cities, my family took trips to Arizona often to visit our relatives that were still there. I was always captivated by the colors and pastels of the desert, the adobe-style architecture, and the creatures and plants that I could never hope to see back home. Kokopelli is a well-known icon representative of the American Southwest, but he originates with the Hopi Native Americans, to whom he is a trickster and fertility god. I had always found images of Kokopelli to be quite eerie for reasons I could never quite articulate; there's just something otherworldly about the desert, and Kokopelli seemed to incapsulate that odd feeling very well.

1904

Despite the growth of both country and engineering feats of our great nation in this exciting generation, Arizona, as I have discovered for myself, is still wild as a feral beast.

It was late May, the weather harsh and unforgiving. My horse, the second and not last to ferry me across the otherworldly state on my expedition, was frothing at the mouth, covered in flies which it no longer had the energy to swat with its whiplike tail. They were attracted to the salty, intimate reek of its sweat, present on its body since the beginning of our ride very early that morning. Starting off just before dawn, I had found, allowed for better mileage, as the unfortunate animal I had conscripted on this journey seemed to take longer to tire if the day's walk began when temperatures and the angle of the sun both were lower.

I pitied the horse, but not nearly as much as I pitied myself. The horse was a means to an end that I could no longer imagine. However, I knew being stranded on the orange hardpan with no company besides the silent Joshua trees and sneaking scorpions was a death sentence. Water was rare, and without an effective means of transportation, I knew I would be dead from the sun, dehydration, or both if left on my own two feet. A dead horse would leave me in this Devil's land to die, after which unimaginable Devils might feel obligated to torture me for eternity, where I guessed I would wander the mesa until the death of time, always thirsty, always dizzy with heat, my sunburned skin bubbling with boils as sweat attempted to break free.

So I stopped my horse and we rested.

Sitting on a rock that burned my sore backside like a brand, the horse's saddle momentarily removed and set aside (much to its relief, I was sure), I removed my once-new pack and took inventory of my rapidly dwindling supplies. The straps scraped across my forearms on its way down, and I hissed in pain. I almost felt I could no longer remember the original color of my skin. It was in a constant cycle of burning, bubbling, burning, bubbling. Opening the pack, I felt for the first time that surely, I was to die in Arizona.

My dried jerky bought in Santa Fe uncountable weeks past was nearly gone, and the apples I thought would hold up well in heat had gone brown days ago. I had been eating them anyway. I had one potato left sporting unappetizing sprouts. I wouldn't bother to cut them off. Every bite counted, no matter what it was. Altogether, I reasoned I had enough food for perhaps another three days.

There were few landmarks in this stretch of Black Mesa. The last river I passed ended abruptly, and I hadn't seen running water in three days. The day before, when I drank the last of my water store from my canteen, I remembered something I heard on some immemorable day in what I now considered to be the before about cactuses holding water.

I'd taken my Bowie knife to the biggest saguaro I could find. It was harder than I thought, and instead of a hollow plant gushing with flowing water, I found a cucumber-like flesh. These flesh pieces, when chewed, were wonderfully refreshing and provided me with hydration, but they did little to ease the scratch in my throat. The horse seemed to understand they were our only option for water now, and obligingly scooped up the chunks of mush I threw at his feet.

My compass and a description of the area were my navigation. My sense of direction had been mostly infallible my entire life, and this route was simple. Start at Memphis, turn west, and go. That's what my brother-in-law said in one of his letters. I'd have to be worse than a half-wit to have trouble.

But Black Mesa does things to your mind.

I was almost sure I was still pointed west, but I was beginning to worry; the heat and unyielding sun might suggest things that aren't there. Since Texas I'd been seeing shimmers on the dusty ground just ahead, but when I came over the hills there wouldn't be a puddle in sight. Sometimes I'd hear rattlers as if they were right in front of me, but the horse gave no indication it heard one of its most feared predators.

I hadn't reached my next landmark, and my feelings of dread were growing. I started hearing whispers in the muffled clop of hooves, in the swish of my riding pants as I walked alongside my horse to give him some rest, in the imagined rattles of nonexistent snakes.

You missed it fifty miles back. Your compass isn't pointing true. You dozed in the saddle and that burden of an animal veered south for two hours.

My rational mind dismissed these thoughts. What else could I do? If I had missed it or gone off course without knowing it, I would get lost if I tried to backtrack. I had to just keep going, step by step, drip by drip of my sweat down my back.

I had to reach civilization at some point.

There wasn't much in terms of proper society in the new territories, but I knew there were lots of people in California, where my brother-in-law awaited my arrival. His trading business was growing, and he knew I was having a hard time of things since my dear Sarah's death, so he'd promised me a job. I saw California on the maps they had hanging at the train station. It only looked a few hundred miles further west. If I kept going, I'd find someone at some point.

God willing, before I starved or cooked to death.

I replaced my sack despite the burning protests of my skin, took a trembling breath, and hoisted the saddle back on my horse.

"Be out of food soon. Maybe we can catch and cook a rattler, eh?"

I'd taken to talking to my horse rather quickly. There was some initial shame at going mad so soon in my ordeal, but I hadn't cared for weeks. It dried my throat something fearsome, but if I went too long without hearing my own voice, I'd start to feel like I didn't exist anymore. As if I was a disembodied soul looking through the eyes of a desert creature, endlessly watching the passing scenery and concerned only with finding my next meal while not becoming one.

Between talking to my horse and my desert-induced hallucinations, not to mention my tattered, filthy, and stinking sun-bleached clothes and my wretched excuse for a hat, I might very well scare away any sort of polite society I would potentially encounter. But I couldn't worry about any of that. Just keep going, step after step after step.

We went for another two hours or so, relishing the evening as the sun finally hid behind the plateaus. I sang a bit of "My Wild Irish Rose" to my horse, but a scratch hit my throat and started a coughing fit halfway through. I chewed on an ear of prickly pear and got it under control.

I stopped us about an hour after sunset and went about removing the saddle and staking my horse. It nosed my pack, likely smelling my rancid apples. A strange warmth gathered in my chest, and I realized I was starting to care for the horse. It didn't have a name, and I hadn't cared enough to check its sex when I paid the last of my money for it in Santa Fe. It seemed pointless after the loss of my first horse, a gentle palomino gelding my brother-in-law had arranged for me. Back then, of course, I'd had the wagon.

The time when I'd had the wagon felt like a past life, a memory barely visible through the haze of my paranoid, almost feral state of mind. The gelding had died partway through Texas. It was unlucky. We were on the ridge of a plateau, and only God knows what spooked him. He shied instinctively to the left, turned his hoof on a loose rock, and went down. The weight of the wagon kept his momentum going, and he went all the way down. I'd been watering the bushes.

As I made my way down the side, he screamed. There's no sound like a horse screaming with mortal pain. About halfway down I remembered my revolver, stuck in my pants and largely forgotten about except at night when the coyotes would howl in the distance. It wasn't a big caliber, just what I could afford, and I was no sharp-shooter. It took almost the entire chamber to put him down. His increasingly frantic screams after each shot echoed in my head at night when I tried to sleep.

Without him to pull the wagon, there wasn't any sense in trying to save my things. Weeping from loss and frustration, I'd turned my back on my father's grandfather clock from Hungary, smartly packed in its box with extra padding, and the fine formal boots my dearly departed Sarah had gifted to me on our wedding day. These were the only things I could keep from the debtors, and they too were taken from me.

My feet had lost most of their skin and I had fever by the time I stumbled into the boarding house of some backwater pueblo a week later. I must've cut a sympathetic figure, as a lovely couple and their two well-behaved children offered me a spot in the back of their wagon. I'd been lucky enough to encounter them on their way to Santa Fe, and they took me that far and hadn't asked anything in return.

I thought about them sometimes as I rode my unnamed horse through the mesa, toward water that wasn't real, away from snakes that only existed in my mind. The children were shy and wide-eyed, but they made sure my blanket stayed wrapped around me in the dead of night when I would toss and turn, casting off nightmares of a screeching horse careening off a cliff straight toward me.

Remembering that gelding, with such a gentle nature and an addiction to carrots, I pulled out a decaying apple and offered it to my horse. He sniffed it gingerly, seemed to reject it, but changed his mind and pulled it from my hand with his whiskery lips.

"Your name is Saguaro," I told him as he munched, and scratched between his ears. His tail, normally lifeless from exhaustion, flicked once.

I had a few bites of my meager food supply, then set down my bedroll and took off my tattered boots. The air was still heavy with heat, so I laid atop my roll and watched the stars move lazily above the desert. They were different here, the stars. At the beginning, I'd found it exciting. Now they made me uneasy. Were they really there, or a trick of the mind like the shining water? Perhaps the heavens had fallen down and unleashed Hell onto the earth, baking it and blistering my skin over and over and over.

That night, the night I gave Saguaro his name, was the first night I heard the flute.

I'd laid down my bedroll a ways up a hill, under a natural shelter made by three rocks grouped together. My sleep was thin, the sounds of the mesa around me always making their way into my strange dreams— a call of a coyote, the scrape of Saguaro's hooves on rock, the cicadas screaming for my attention. The nights in the desert could be very cold, and the bite of its cruel teeth would linger on my skin through the night, only to be melted like ice once the boiling sun rose.

That night, through the thin haze of my restless sleep, I began to hear a strange sound from somewhere far away. My dream was mostly abstract shapes and colors, and when the sound began, the colors turned fearful, malicious, rotten.

What finally pulled me from sleep was a whinny from Saguaro. I'd staked him in the dirt, nearby but far enough that he wouldn't step on me in my sleep, a pathetic sage-colored shrub of dry vegetation within reach of his flat teeth.

I looked around, disoriented as always upon waking, and saw him a few feet away, ears pinned back. He whinnied again and scraped at the dirt with his front hoof.

I stood, shaking myself free of my fraying blanket.

"Here, here, Saguaro, what's the matter?" I said soothingly, walking over to him and putting my hand under his whiskery lips for him to sniff.

His black, wet nostrils flared at my scent and he pushed his nose against my hand, grunting. He flicked his tail back and forth at nothing.

"Something out there?" I asked, his body language making me nervous.

I strained my ears, focusing in on the sound that I'd just noticed followed me from my dream. It sounded very far away, but sound traveled strangely in the mesa. I followed it for a few moments, amazed.

It was a melody.

It sounded not quite like any instrument I'd heard before, but the closest thing I could think of was a wind or reed instrument, a huge flute that moved so much air the space around it would vibrate.

I hadn't built a fire that night, nor for the last several. I had no wood, and the dry plants of the desert resisted most of my sparks. I could start fires with it, but it was usually a long hassle and I didn't have the energy for it. Without the light of a fire, my eyes were well adjusted to the inky blackness of the night. I gazed down the meager hill where I'd set up camp.

I saw nothing in the darkness but Joshua trees and clumps of that wiry brush, as well as a fair amount of rocks in all sizes. The land here was mostly flat, a few small hills here and there. It was very different from where I'd first entered Arizona, the high plateaus lining both sides of me as if I was the current of a giant invisible river.

The music seemed to be coming from the south, though I didn't pull out my compass to make sure.

Surely, if there was music, there were people to make it.

The thought of seeing another person filled me with elation. The melody brightened, the notes soaring higher in pitch. I rose with it, my soul reaching south for comfort.

I didn't care that it was the middle of the night; I needed to speak to something that would understand and speak back.

I pulled on my boots and cracked leather coat, taking eager steps toward where my hill began to slope down. Sand fluttered around my feet and the soles of my boots scraped against rock.

Then the howling began.

I stopped cold, the smile dropping from my sun-cracked face.

Wolves, from the sound, were somewhere near where the music was coming from. Their howls told me there were at least three, maybe four.

Almost as if in response to their cries, the flute increased in volume.

I was frozen, listening with such intense focus that I jumped when the coyotes joined in.

Their short, clipped yips added a staccato to the melody, and I realized that the animals of the desert were creating harmonies, pleasing to the ear but somehow urgent, insistent, that complemented the flute.

The music was otherworldly, like something I shouldn't be here to witness. The flute became louder, not from more effort but proximity. It seemed to be coming nearer to my camp.

Wolves howled and coyotes yipped, and I thought I heard the harsh bark of hyenas. All these animal voices moved with the flute, coming near.

Coming to my camp.

When I realized that a number of nocturnal predators were heading in my direction, I shook the frost from my feet and scrambled for my bags, which I had laid up against one of the rocks that made up my shelter. I yanked my revolver free of the worn leather with a shaking hand.

The music was beautiful, but it was also dangerous. An undercurrent of warning, danger, dread flowed just beneath. It made me feel *red* inside. Like rot just beginning to smell in the desert heat. I could smell something like ripe carrion drifting toward me in the wind.

Clutching the revolver in one hand, I turned and scrambled up onto the rocks that created my windbreak. I knew the revolver wasn't guaranteed protection; it was loaded with six bullets, the rest of my meager cache stashed in my bags. Six bullets, even if shot with good aim, which I knew I didn't possess, would hardly be enough for an entire pack of wolves or hyenas, especially if they all attacked at once.

Still, its heavy, cold weight in my palm was reassuring as I settled in a tense crouch on top of the rocks. Being higher up made me feel safer too. I heard something from my right, but it was only Saguaro's hooves scraping against the hardpan.

I realized the kind thing to do would be to untie him, if a pack of wolves was truly headed this way. It would be cruel to leave him tethered with nowhere to run, but once I was in the perceived safety of my roost, I felt as though I couldn't move, that the second my boot touched down on the dirt, the wolves would appear.

"Sorry, buddy," I whispered to him.

My eyes were glued in the direction of the music, louder now with every minute. My heart hammered in my ears as I crouched, stock still, searching for signs of movement in the desert. I could make out the Joshuas, the shrubs, the cactuses. No animals that I could see were flitting between cover.

The way sound traveled in the desert was deceptive, I knew, but the music was so loud it sounded like it should've been right there, at the base of my hill.

I watched, barely blinking, as the dark shape that had been a Joshua just a moment before suddenly shifted. I started reflexively, and had to clamp my left hand over my mouth for fear I'd cry out.

The shape, too black for my eyes to define, moved with excruciating slowness across the bottom of my hill. While it had originally been the size and shape of the surrounding Joshuas, it now lengthened before my eyes, standing far above seven feet tall.

The clouds had been creeping in for some time, pushed by the night winds, and I realized this as the light from the moon dimmed. I could still see the shape, moving in strange, weaving lines at the base of the hill, but any hope of making out more details disappeared with the moon's light.

My head was aching from the music, the sheer noise of it, the screams of the invisible nocturnal beasts in their beautiful, forbidden melody. Incorporeal fingers tickled up my spine as I shook, frozen with fear atop the rocks, waiting for the predators to pass like a rabbit in a burrow.

I don't know how long I crouched up there, my calves and knees aching and burning from holding the position, watching the inhumanly tall shape stalk back and forth, like it could smell me.

After some time, the music began to fade in volume, moving away from my camp. It sounded amused, like it knew I had been hiding but didn't bother to come scare me from my burrow.

Like it knew there was no hurry; it would get to me in its own time.

I woke with a start the next morning, curled up under my blankets. When had I crawled back down from the rocks? I didn't have any memory of it.

Saguaro looked at me judgmentally as I rose from my roll, bones creaking and joints popping. His earlier nervousness was gone; he lowered his head back down, disinterested, and nibbled on the dry shrub below.

After I packed up my camp, I consulted my compass and set out for the day.

As I put miles behind me and that windbreak of rocks, the hot sun burning the chill from my bones, the memory of the night before took on an easier shape to understand.

It had been a dream. Vivid, terrifying, but not real.

I'd checked around the base of the hill before throwing myself onto Saguaro and leaving. No animal prints, no dung, certainly no signs that the Joshuas had ever been anything but.

I'd had vivid dreams before, especially in the month after losing Sarah. I'd see her floating above me where I slept, her face pale and sickly, like it had been in the last days before the sickness took her from me. I could even hear her voice and smell her hair.

But I knew they were dreams while I was in them.

This had felt so real. It had carried none of that feeling of unreality that filled those dreams of Sarah.

But it couldn't have been real. There was no one around for miles, maybe even a hundred miles for all I knew.

Nothing that lived out here in the desert could play an instrument like that, so I dismissed it from my mind, where it faded but lingered somewhere in the shadows.

Saguaro died five days later.

I knew the lack of proper food had been wearing away at him for a long time, but the only food I could offer him was long gone, the brown apples having been finished off days before. I had resorted to catching and cooking scorpions and snakes, which was difficult when my movements were so slowed from hunger. With the snakes, the trick was to catch them in their underground burrows while they slept during the day. I was bitten the first few times, which hurt horribly, but were evidently not laced with venom, as I experienced no ill effects aside from the pain.

Scorpions were harder to catch, but when I did, I savored the crunch beneath my teeth. Surviving in the wild was full of a surprising amount of dull, unsatisfying foods like cactuses and wild grasses. When I crunched the scorpions, cooked first in hard-won brush campfires, I imagined they were seared potato skins, crispy bacon, or even the crunch of the tortillas I'd eaten in Santa Fe.

Saguaro, however, was an herbivore, and would not partake in these meals. He ate the scrubby weeds and sparse dry grasses in the area, but the energy he expended carrying me across the mesa was simply too much to replace with what they could provide him.

He collapsed while I was taking a break from riding, sitting on a rock and chewing on the meat of a cactus. He looked at me, his eye barely open in a slit, with accusation. This wouldn't have happened if not for me. I knew it.

So I crouched by his head, scratching between his ears and murmuring comfort as his life drained away.

When his massive sides stopped rising, I wept.

Some time later, maybe three days, maybe a week, I looked up and saw a very detailed hallucination before me.

I'd been the very picture of madness alone on the boiling hardpan; I chattered to myself, sang songs, and cried intermittently. I wasn't hungry anymore; my stomach had shriveled in on itself, a useless weight in my midsection, where I could now feel the hard ridges of my ribs under my skin.

I now heard the flute music during the day; it flitted into and out of my awareness as the miles slowly stretched behind my dragging, blistered feet.

During the day, there were no wolves or coyotes or hyenas adding harmony; just the melody of the instrument flitting around in my head like a butterfly.

At night, however, it was so close I could feel the air blown around by the flute against the skin of my cracked and bleeding face. The wolves would howl, the coyotes would yip, and the hyenas would laugh as I lay with my eyes screwed shut, petrified with fear and not daring to look at the dark shape I knew was right above me. Precious water escaped my body as I cried with terror.

I knew it wasn't real; I knew I had gone mad.

I'd heard it said that madness is never apparent to the truly insane man, but the things I saw in the mesa couldn't have been real, and I knew it. Once, I'd glanced to my right and found a diamondback rattlesnake beside me, slithering its way through the sand in that strange body wave, keeping perfect pace with me, as if we were on an after-dinner stroll in the city.

The flute music wasn't really there, but I heard it constantly. It still invoked in me the sense of rot and decay, and sometimes, if I looked from the corner of my eye, I thought I could see that seven-foot-tall shape walking just behind me, the shape that had formed and lengthened from the Joshua tree in that horrifying vivid dream.

Sometimes Sarah walked beside me, her straw-colored hair blowing in a desert wind that wasn't any more real than her, the long tresses freed scandalously from her usual updo, like it was when we were alone in our bedroom at night, her body clinging to mine. She never spoke or looked at me, but her presence gave me comfort. She was a relief compared to that lumbering black shape blowing its haunting melody in my ear.

I knew I would probably die soon from exposure. This idea I could accept. Sarah waited for me on the other side, so close to that curtain that I could feel her reaching her palm toward me through it, pushing the shape of it into the fabric. I just hoped I died before that shape finally emerged from my the edge of my vision, before I gave in and opened my eyes to look at the thing that hovered right over my face at night while I feigned sleep.

These visions had caused me to accept my madness, so the hallucination that unrolled before me on that day was no surprise at all.

A group of buildings, made from the elements of the surrounding mesa, were arranged in a rough circle, the center of which moved and thrummed with bodies of dark, leathery skin. I couldn't hear anything besides the ringing in my ears from the sun, but I imagined they were speaking, laughing, singing. A girl sat against a wall and turned a figure over in her small hands. It looked like a strange doll, its face black as coal and feathers adorning its body.

I drank in the hallucination thirstily, the strange humanoid shapes a comfort in my final dying breaths.

My body collapsed onto the desert floor, and my last sensation was of urgent voices in the distance, coming closer. I thought of the flute and that first night it had come so near with its contingent of wolves, coyotes and hyenas, knowing I was there, hiding like a rabbit.

It had finally come for me, and I closed my eyes as it grabbed hold of me, not wanting to behold its terrible form.

Something was over my eyes.

I still have eyes? I thought.

In the darkness, my mind flailed. Was this death? I could see nothing, no Sarah, no angels. I did hear voices, but their words were undiscernible and distant.

My hand twitched, for I did have hands still, and reached up. I tried to touch my eyes, but there was something blocking my fingers from touching the skin. It was warm and wet. I grabbed at it, suddenly fearful that a rodent had laid over my face and died, bleeding into my eye sockets.

I grabbed it and thrust it away, the darkness vanishing. My eyes tried to open and were met with resistance. Someone spoke from what sounded like another room, the tones male and urgent.

I touched my eyelids and pried them open with my fingertips, the goopy crust of desert sand giving way under the force.

I was in some sort of dwelling. The walls were the color of the mesa outside, the floor dirt. It was hot, still, but indirectly, my skin being protected from the direct sun by the roof. I was laying in the corner, on a bed of blankets, their colorful woven patterns dizzying to my heat-addled mind.

"Hello?" I croaked, the flesh of my throat burning from dryness.

The door in the dwelling, made of wood and primitive-looking, swung open, and the desert air whooshed in. A man entered, his skin swarthy and cracked like old leather. His hair, ink-black, was contained beneath a strip of cloth tied around his head. He wore no shirt, and a cloth dyed turquoise and red, etched with patterns along the bottom, was wrapped around his hips. He wore necklaces of leather strung with white and red beads. I guessed he could be anywhere from his forties to sixties.

The man came straight to me, a strip of damp cloth laid over an arm and a clay bowl of smelly, smashed herbs in one hand, a bowl of steaming food in the other, and a tin cup balanced in the crook of his arm. He approached me with a bored air, glancing at the cloth I'd thrown from my eyes, which lay limply on the dirt.

He clicked his tongue, shook his head, and murmured something incomprehensible.

"Who are you?" I asked, my voice thin as a cobweb. "Where am I?"

The man sat in a wooden chair beside my bed, setting down his load carefully, and scooped up some of the herbs with his fingers. He held them up to my face.

They smelled terrible, like worms and moldy bread. I moved my head away in reaction.

"Eat," the man said. His voice was deep and commanding.

"What is it?" I asked, looking into his dark brown eyes.

"Medicine," he said, and pushed his fingers to my mouth.

I opened my lips and let him scrape the herbs onto my tongue, feeling like a child.

They tasted much worse than they smelled, but I swallowed them anyway, holding my breath.

"Who are you?" I repeated.

"I am Kwahu."

The man set down the bowl and grabbed the new cloth, dabbing my forehead. I sat up, and he looked at me with patient irritation.

"Where am I?" I asked, then began coughing as the dryness tore at my throat.

Kwahu handed me the tin cup, and I drank eagerly. The water was fresh and cool, evidently from a well. I drained it in three gulps and handed it back.

"Oraibi is our village," Kwahu answered after taking the cup from me.

"Do you all speak English?" I asked.

"Some. Not everyone wanted to learn. The Mormons taught me, so I could read their holy book. You were in the desert long time," he said with no upward inflection, making it sound like a statement rather than a question.

"Yes," I answered. "I'm going to California."

"With no horse? That is death," he said.

"I had one. I had a whole wagon, in the beginning. My horse was killed in a fall, and the one I had after that just died a few days ago." I looked around, suddenly alarmed. "My bags- where are my bags?"

Kwahu reached behind his chair and held up my worn leather bags, brushed with sand.

"Your things are safe. Gun too."

I relaxed again and coughed a little.

"We found you outside Oraibi, on the ground. Thought you were dead. Not enough water."

He picked up the steaming bowl and handed it to me wordlessly. He watched me eat.

"This is delicious," I said earnestly, shoveling it into my dry mouth. "What is it?"

"Noqkwivi," he answered bluntly, then chided, "Eat slower. You will be sick."

When I finished, unabashedly licking the plate clean, I looked at Kwahu.

"Thank you for helping me. You saved my life."

His expression did not change. "Is what makes us Hopi. You are welcome as long as needs. Drink and eat and have medicine, then go to California."

"Thank you, Kwahu."

I let my crusted eyes wander around the kiva. They came to rest on the strange figures that filled the shelf on the wall.

"What are those sculptures?" I asked. "They are very nice."

"Kachinas," Kwahu answered in that emotionless way of his. "Messengers of spirit world. White men buy them for art."

The figures, each one different from the last, were painted with black, turquoise, red and yellow, and feathers were glued to their heads. Some held little carved staffs, some had heads that resembled birds or beasts. I'd been staring at them most of my waking moments, drinking in their colors and craftsmanship.

They were fascinating but frightening, in an odd way. Their animal-like faces painted in the bright colors of the mesa reminded me of the nocturnal calls of unseen animals accompanied by that menacing flute. One was even made to look like a wolf-man, tufts of white hair glued around the head, a snout and ears poking out from it. It had beady black eyes that unnerved me, seeming to watch me intently.

There were painted wooden carvings on the walls, some depicting men or animals, others simply decorated with angular abstract lines.

One painting in particular caught my attention.

It was man-shaped, a black illustration on the light wood. It had lines sprouting from its head, indicating hair. Its knees were bent and it held a long, straight object in its hands, holding it up to its head. My heart began to hammer against my chest as I beheld it.

"What is that?" I asked, forcing my throat to make the sounds.

"That is Kokopelli," Kwahu answered gravely. "It is his season. He is mischief, tricks. Also new life and music."

My lips were numb. "Music?"

"Mm."

"What is that in his hands?" I asked, already knowing the answer.

"Flute," he said, looking at the painting with reverence. "Kokopelli plays flute."

For Grandmother

SATURNALIA

I wrote this quick and nasty piece for Pen & Sword as a holiday "gift". I didn't want to do the classic festive horror— Santa slasher, Krampus— so I did some research into the Roman holiday Saturnalia, the essential precursor to what we celebrate now as Christmas. Be warned, this story is short but not sweet. Maybe don't eat while reading it.

Eshmun sat at the Senator's banquet table. He wore fine clothes dyed rich blues and purples, colors he hadn't worn in years. Not since his capture.

The Senator himself strode into the room, his clothing bright and unstained.

"*Io*, Saturnalia!" The Senator cried with merry delight.

Eshmun stirred in the plush chair, uncomfortable. The Romans were a strange people, and they lived so loudly. Their customs and culture were still alien to him even after five years of living among them, serving them, scrubbing the floors after galas, the sour vomit smell never quite washing off his calloused hands.

The Senator smiled and snapped his soft fingers. "First course!"

Ten of Eshmun's master's fellow Senators emerged through the door leading to the culina, where all the Senator's meals were prepared, their hands which have never known true work gripping beautiful silver serving platters. The plates were piled high with steaming confections of every kind imaginable: roast mutton that dripped with savory fat and oil, candied fruits, loaves of rich dark bread sliced and served with *bowls* full of butter.

Eshmun's ears rang with the noise of the dining hall. The other slaves were enraptured by the beautiful clothes, the new shoes, the lush décor and table settings of fine silver. But all this opulence made Eshmun nervous.

Surely such treatment of slaves is illegal, he thought, wincing as the new leather of his gifted shoes pinched his crooked toe. *Any moment he will turn angry and have us whipped for wearing such things, for sitting at his table.*

The Senators, laughing and teasing one another, delighted in a moment of living life from the other side, setting the food down across the ridiculous length of the table. Eshmun and the rest of the Senator's slaves eyed the food with longing but did not reach out and touch it.

"Today is the first day of Saturnalia," the Senator boomed, "My fellow Senators and I humbly serve you in keeping with tradition. I understand that many of you are from other lands where this may seem strange. It is customary for masters to serve their slaves during Saturnalia, a day for celebration and chaos as we honor Saturn. Please, enjoy yourselves."

At this, the other slaves reached greedily for the food, their normally filthy hands scrubbed clean in the bathing rooms an hour before. Eshmun felt as though his master did not view him and the other slaves as humans, rather as playthings to dress up and set around like children play with clay figures.

As the slaves plopped piles of steaming food onto their shining plates, the giggling Senators approached the table again with freshly uncorked wine, pouring it into the slaves' sparkling clean glasses with gusto. Glasses that the slaves had washed themselves only the night before after one of their master's gluttonous parties.

How these Romans love their wine, Eshmun thought, his nose wrinkling. Something about the entire show rankled him. It was a joke to these high-society Romans, pretending he and his fellow slaves were people for a night, giggling and miming such activities as scrubbing the floors and beating rugs.

It was all just fun to them. And Eshmun decided he didn't want to dance around and put on a grateful face for them, make them feel like gracious gods for a night.

He sat in the chair, wearing the fine clothes and ridiculous shoes that pinched his toe, but he sat with arms crossed, not touching the food, the wine, or even the water, even though the feast set before him was more food than he'd ever seen in one place his entire life.

He would not participate in this Saturnalia.

They can sack my city and enslave me and my people, but they cannot make me into a plaything if I do not let them, Eshmun thought with satisfaction.

He glanced at the group of Senators, who had quieted their antics and now watched the slaves imbibe in food and drink like they were actors on a stage. Their attention was rapt, excited.

Anticipatory.

What are they…

Then the coughing began.

No.

Several slaves around the table fell from their chairs, their mouths spewing barely-chewed mutton and pastries and rank wine all over themselves, the table, the floor. They started to shake, collapsing fully onto the ornate tiles of the floor and twitching, their heads and heels drumming. The room filled with the stench of the dying, of stomach acid and lining and the liquid contents of destroyed bowels.

A sound rose above the choked cries and moans and thuds of seizing limbs.

Laughing.

Eshmun turned and saw the Senators. They watched the horrific, inhuman scene with mirth, clutching their stomachs and wiping at their eyes. He watched one of the men retch and vomit onto his expensive tunic, the brightly dyed fabric stained with the browns and yellows of the man's latest decadent meal. He was not poisoned as well, Eshmun realized, simply unable to hold his gorge among the depravity. The man continued to bellow laughter as the vomit dried on his front.

Eshmun stood from the table in shock and horror. The chair *clacked* to the floor behind him, and he spun about wildly. What could he do? Three-quarters of the slaves in the dining hall already lay still on the rich tiles, breathing their last as their bodily fluids coagulated beneath them. He could not save them, his fellow oppressed, many of which in this very room he had known back in Carthage, back before the Romans came and overpowered their great city.

Before they took them back to their grand estates with marble pillars and monstrous tapestries only to murder them on a day set aside for chaos and mischief.

The Senators saw him and roared with laughter, pointing and clutching themselves. Just then, a slave seized and fell forward onto the table, knocking a silver candelabra over on its side. The flames caught on the tablecloth, reaching a spot of spilled fat from a dead slave's plate and igniting it with a *whoosh.*

The Senators clapped and cheered at the sight. The chaos and misery fed them like starving children on the streets.

The flames crawled across the table, licking up every drop of fat and oil and spilled wine. It reached the body of a woman with long braids, her face having fallen into her stew bowl when she collapsed, and the braids lit up like kindling. The smell of her charring flesh mingled with the sour reek of the vomit, and that was when Eshmun finally vomited himself, coating the ridiculous leather shoes in his slave rations served to him the night before. Cabbage soup without any salt.

The fire had spread across the entire table, and the wood quickly collapsed under the damage, spilling everything to the floor and spreading the flames in a pool. They engulfed more of the bodies, most of them now lying still.

Eshmun was the only one of them still alive. All others had eaten the poisoned food. Allowed their dignities to be quashed in this twisted, childish game.

The Senators did not look overworried about Eshmun's survival. They bolted in a line of guffaws for the double doors, escaping and closing them behind themselves. Eshmun ran to the doors after them, but as he neared, he heard scraping and smacking from outside, saw the doors being jostled.

Eshmun knew they were trapping him in here with the grotesquerie of ruptured human bodies. He tried the doors anyway, shoving against them with his entire body's weight.

The doors did not budge. Eshmun heard the Senators cackle at his attempt.

Smoke began to fill the dining hall, and Eshmun choked as he breathed in the reek of burning bodies. *I'm going to die in here.*

Then he remembered. He'd served meals here before on occasion when his master had executed the usual staff for serving dissatisfactory meals.

The servant's door. It led to the culina, which had to a door to the gardens.

Escape.

Eshmun turned and sprinted across the room, coughing and wincing at the smoke that assailed his eyes, nose and mouth. His foot, still clad in the now-filthy leather shoe, slipped on a puddle of vomit and Eshmun went sprawling, falling hard on his hands and right knee. He pulled himself up, too shaken to feel the pain as his knee began to bleed, and stumbled through the room to the small door in the far wall.

Part of him, the part that had been enslaved and beaten and treated like filth, expected the Senators to have blocked this door as well. But the gods smiled upon Eshmun in that moment. The door fell open under his shove and he went to his knees again in the culina, crying out as the split skin on his knee opened wider.

Eshmun made for the back door, bowed over in pain, and fell into it with desperate force. It gave way and then he was outside, the fresh, cold night air filling his nose and cleared it of the reek of his burning brethren.

Eshmun took off sprinting into the dark countryside, no regard for a destination other than *away* from his depraved master and the sickening laughter of his fellow Senators.

He made it over five hundred *pedes* before he began screaming from the horror he had witnessed.

For Clara, who encouraged me to be as gross as possible in my flash

NO ONE EVER SEES ME

This story was heavily inspired by a story told to me by my friend, Dungeon Master and Budo Taijuitsu instructor, Dustin Alexander. It's more of a sitting-on-rockers-on-the-porch kind of story, and it's a bit short, but it's dear to me. It was first published in the September 2025 issue of Dark Harbor Magazine, now Macabre Magazine.

Every Halloween, my cousins and I played Ninjas.

Our grandmother had ten children. Ten children all got married except Uncle Steve. He died in Vietnam, and my dad always poured a beer into the grass for Uncle Steve when all the siblings got together. The remaining nine siblings all had at least one child with their spouses before a slew of divorces, remarriages, and one spouse lost to cancer.

All these children having children is what led to The Cousins, a term we said with reverence, with importance, when we referred to all these children of the nine siblings. With an age range spanning nearly thirty years, there were forty-three of us. Practically a battalion.

Halloween was the best family event of the year.

Some families only get together on Christmas, or Thanksgiving, or maybe not at all. But there were simply too many of us for one Thanksgiving dinner, one gift-opening session around a dry evergreen. There was no house big enough for all of us to gather.

Until Aunt Lydia and Uncle Joel bought The Farm, another proper noun to us Cousins, our large number contributing to our sense of importance, of unity. The Cousins gathered at The Farm, where we would play games.

The Farm was twenty acres of a child's wildest dreams. Endless trees to climb, fields to explore, hills to roll down giggling, and even a creek to wade in during the summer months, to walk across at Christmas and pretend we were in *The Lion, The Witch and the Wardrobe.*

It also sported a massive barn that, to our extreme delight, was rotting, unused, and full of places to hide.

While we invented and played many games as The Cousins, the most fun, we all agreed (except Lainie, who pretended to be too old for games), was Ninjas.

Ninjas started in the barn as hide and seek, the old farming equipment, rotting hay bales bleached white with age, and junk-stuffed hayloft providing a myriad of perfect hiding spots for us. The barn was nearly the size of the main farmhouse, huge and cavernous, full of what a child saw as treasure, adventure. None of us minded the smell of mildew and dust. I still believe those smells are the best in the world at inspiring the imagination.

Jamie tries to take credit for the idea that turned hide and seek into something more "sophisticated", the white flags and total darkness that made the game our own. I don't remember who actually had the idea, but I *know* it wasn't Jamie. He was the smoke blower of The Cousins. Last year he tried to convince me his girlfriend was a famous OnlyFans creator. You know the type.

Regardless of whose idea it really was, hide and seek in the barn turned into Ninjas by the third year of The Farm. It was our special game, and we only played on Halloween.

Some of the younger Cousins would try to convince us to play at other times of the year. I didn't blame them; the game was a great time. We never caved though, whether it was Christmas, Easter, or Fourth of July.

Ninjas was strictly a Halloween game, and we stuck to it.

It was perfect for the spooky season, an event that all us Cousins looked forward to. Halloween to some kids meant candy, dressing up, watching scary movies. To us Cousins, it meant playing Ninjas. All that other stuff was secondary.

The last time I ever played Ninjas, I was sixteen.

Most teenagers lose their interest in kid games around the time they gain interest in sex, but The Cousins had too tight of a bond to be broken by a false sense of maturity. Kelly, twenty-seven at the time, still played every year with enthusiasm. So, being my age and still playing was not unusual.

That year was like any other, all of us showing up at The Farm with our black outfits and face chalk, excited and full of energy. We passed the time and watched the sun set anxiously as the nine siblings, spouses in tow, drank wine and discussed the latest scandals.

The energy among us was palpable by eight o'clock, the sun teasing us by throwing out its very last light in a desperate attempt to keep our game at bay.

Our parents finally released us outside at nine thirty, likely very late for the younger Cousins, but holidays were always exceptions. We congregated around the front of the barn in the new black night, all of us in our darkest clothing, black lines painted under our eyes like football players. Kelly and I were nominated to be the "flashlight holders" and had been for several years running.

If any Cousins got lost, scared, or otherwise needed to be escorted from the pitch-darkness of the barn, the flashlight holders were to guide them out into the fresh October night air. The four light bars that hung on rusty chains from the barn roof still worked, amazingly, but were flicked off for the game. We needed utter blackness.

That year, as we waited for the rest of us to gather, my eyes landed on Caleb, the youngest Cousin (at least until someone else had another kid). Caleb was six, still young enough to inst-inctively reach for my hand as he sidled up to me.

"Hey Caleb," I said, taking his small hand. The gesture made me feel warm despite the late October chill.

"I'm scared," Caleb said in his small voice. "I don't like the dark."

This was Caleb's first year playing Ninjas; his mother, Aunt Jen, had forbidden it every year before. She ranted about rusty machinery and tetanus shots, a sentiment long worn out by the other adults. The argument was a lost cause and they knew it, but Aunt Jen had been adamant. Until this year, it seemed.

"Hey, you'll be okay, buddy. It's really, really fun," I assured him, bending to my knees to talk face to face with him. "Plus, if you really get too scared, me and Kelly have magic flashlights."

"Magic?"

"Yeah, see?" I said, and clicked mine on. I shined it at the dying grass beneath our feet. "It can guide us out of the barn, no matter how scared or lost we are."

Caleb's face melted into a crooked smile. His front teeth were missing. "Oh. Okay. That's good."

I straightened and tousled his hair, fond of the boy. We'd gathered at The Farm for his first birthday, a riotous celebration, and the maternally inclined female cousins doted on him every chance they got. His cherubic face and sweet innocence made us all melt.

The last of the participating Cousins arrived, absorbing teasing remarks from the more brash of us. Twenty in all this year. A good turnout. Despite the popularity of the game, it was very rare for every single Cousin to be present at a gathering. Families went on vacations, had busy work schedules, got sick.

As flashlight holders, Kelly and I were the informal leaders of the game. I clapped my hands twice for silence, and all eyes were on me.

"This is Caleb's first time playing, so I wanted to go over the rules," I said loudly, projecting my voice over the small crowd of relatives. "There are ten white flags hidden throughout the barn. Your goal is to grab a flag and keep it, moving quietly and without being seen. If you are found by another player, they can take your flag and you're out. Remember, if you can't find your way out of the barn, shout for me or Kelly and we'll guide you." I brandished my flashlight for effect. "At the end of half an hour, we turn on the lights. Whoever has a flag when the lights come on is a winner. Any questions?"

A rumbling wave of negatory responses flowed from the crowd of Cousins.

"Alright. Let's play Ninjas!"

The Cousins poured into the barn, spreading out and muttering excitedly amongst themselves. By the time everyone was inside and in position, barely two minutes had passed. We took Ninjas seriously.

Caleb was still hovering near me as I gave Kelly a nod. "Remember," I muttered down to him, "I'm here if you need me."

Caleb smiled at me and nodded.

"Ready!" I called out across the barn. My voice sounded flat against the rotting boards. I cranked the kitchen timer borrowed from Aunt Lydia and set it to *30*. "Lights out!"

Kelly flipped the master switch, and the meager light bars flicked out with relief. We were pitched into sudden complete blackness, the only hint of light from a few stars visible where boards had fallen off the walls. Barely a rustle was heard, a tiny creak of wood. We were good at Ninjas. We knew how to walk quietly, how to use the darkest shadows to our advantage. An actual practitioner of ninpō would've been impressed at our skill.

I backed up and sat beside a wheelbarrow filled with twigs and rainwater from the leaking roof. The hay poked into my black sweatpants. I didn't notice it. I was listening. Watching.

The tick of the kitchen timer was loud, marching band loud in the dead silence of the barn. I didn't even hear Caleb blundering around, assumedly unskilled at the art of moving quietly. I was impressed.

A few minutes later, I heard a surprised grunt and an irritated grumble from the northwest section of the barn, up in the hayloft. Our first ninja had been eliminated.

I listened for my name, ready in case my flashlight and guidance were needed. No such call came, and the heavy barn doors to my right opened briefly for a moment, then thudded closed.

My legs grew numb as I sat waiting by the wheelbarrow. Eventually I had to adjust my position, making no noise against the hay as I uncrossed and refolded my tingling legs.

At one point, someone passed almost right in front of me. It was impossible to say who, but I heard the gentle, slow but steady footfalls of someone in the hay. They had likely just acquired a flag and were anxious to tuck into a good hiding spot, not wanting to get caught in the open with their new prize. I smiled and shook my head as the footfalls landed, silently chiding the Cousin for stepping toes first instead of heel-to-toe, the silent way of walking explained to us by Rob, who claimed to have read several books on the art of ninpō two summers before.

I had to clap a hand over my mouth as the tiny, barely perceptible sound of a second set of feet passed where the loud Cousin had been only moments before. They were caught, I knew it. Giggles bubbled up from my chest, barely restrained.

As expected, a grunt of surprise and a murmured tease sounded some twenty feet ahead as the Cousin was caught. There was some back and forth, a hushed argument over the fairness of the tag, which was like shouting in the silence of the blackened barn.

I stood, knees cracking even at my young age, and prepared to break up the argument for the sake of our sacred silence. But before I could click on my flashlight, the bright referee of this game, someone plodded loudly through the hay past me and threw open the barn door, not caring about making noise any longer. Poor sport.

There was little incident after that. My internal clock was imprecise but close, and I began to suspect the timer was almost out. The barn doors had opened and closed eight times.

In the black silence of the barn, the rotting smell was long since filtered out by my nose. The barn, to me, smelled of Halloween, of family, of the love of a great game. I wondered, for the first time at my young age, how much longer the magic of Halloween would last. My mother told me often that holidays lose their shine when you become an adult, and that they only become special again once you've got kids.

The idea of Halloween losing its shine was suddenly terrifying to me. In the dark, my heart sped up. How do you know when it's the last time you feel that childlike wonder of imagination? My father said once that, at some point in my life, he picked me up and set me down for the very last time, and he never knew it.

Was this Halloween, this game of Ninjas, my last time being picked up? I wanted to cry at the thought.

A hand slid into mine.

I narrowly avoided screaming in the black silence.

The hand was small and sweaty, familiar. Caleb. Yes, that was Caleb. I could hear him breathing softly next to me. He had gotten scared, so late in the game it was almost tragic. I tightened my hand around his tiny one.

I thought of his approaching adolescence, of the wonders it would hold, of the way he might remember this first game of Ninjas for the rest of his life, going over it again and again like he was handling an old, worn photograph. At this thought, I did cry. A single tear escaped my right eye, seen by no one in the dark.

Caleb was right next to me, his mouth level with my ear as I sat in the hay. I could feel the moisture from his breath on my neck. I shivered.

When I whispered to Caleb, my voice was thick.

"Hey, buddy. You're a great ninja, I didn't even see you coming," I praised, hoping to instill him with confidence in his childish fear.

Then Caleb spoke in a voice that was strangely glum, mournful.

"No one ever sees me."

My brow wrinkled. I opened my mouth to ask what he meant by that and just then, the kitchen timer buzzed in my lap, causing me to jump. It was like a fire alarm in the silent barn.

Kelly immediately flipped on the master switch and I heard cries of pain across the barn as our eyes burned in the sudden brightness of the ancient lights.

It only took me a second to recover, but when I looked back down at Caleb, he wasn't there.

I didn't hear him slip away, didn't feel his hand leaving mine. My palm was still sticky with his sweat.

But he was gone, as if he'd vanished as soon as he'd spoken.

"What?" I whispered to myself, looking all around me for any sign of him.

Then the kids with white flags were hoisting them victoriously in the air, cheering and already talking animatedly about the game, describing close calls, near blunders.

My eyes flicked up as I saw a small figure emerge from the depths of the hay loft, on the opposite side of the barn from me.

It was Caleb.

He was hoisting a white flag, a look of rabid pride and victory on his cherubic face.

"I got one, Nathan! See!" He was calling to me, and I could only stare as I realized there was no way he could've gotten so far so fast.

No one ever sees me.

Who was that breathing near me, holding my hand?

For Dusty

BABYDOLL

I originally wrote this story as a flash exercise— I wanted to combine the horror genre with a random one in a piece. I ended up with romance as my second genre, and while this story doesn't specifically strike as a gooey steam piece, I think there's really no truer love than a love that endures despite age, time, and the fog of degenerative disease. I made myself cry when I wrote this piece, so I hope it tugs on your emotions as well. That's the entire goal of art, after all. Babydoll was first published in the December 2025 issue of Tumbleweird and was edited to perfection by Lari.

Tom looked around him, blinking. He did not understand what he was seeing — a small, cramped room, with hardwood floors and olive green walls. A bureau sat against the wall opposite him, a tiny television hanging above it. There was art on the walls — bland depictions of boats on pastel blue water, lighthouses with flocks of birds in the sky. He did not recognize any of them.

This was not his bedroom.

Tom's bedroom had brown carpet and cedar plank walls, decorated with three of his favorite impressionist pieces, collected over the years from the art fairs he and his wife, Rita, loved to wander together. It sat inside the single-story rambler they had purchased three years ago with the money he'd earned from the construction company he had built to profitability from the ground up.

Tom ran his hands over the soft, puffy arms of the chair he was sitting in — an armchair patterned with navy blue and beige stripes. Tom did not have an armchair in his bedroom, and certainly would not have chosen one so tasteless and sterile as this. The fabric felt cheap and worn, and static built up under his palm as he rubbed it.

He lifted his wrist to check the time, but his watch was gone. *Weird.*

"Rita!" he called. He felt a sudden urge to see his wife right now.

Tom stood up, his knees wobbly, and walked to the television to inspect it more closely. It was incredibly small and thin, hardly stuck out from the wall at all. He had never seen anything like it.

"Rita! Come look at this thing!"

Have I travelled to the future? The thought made him chuckle — ridiculous, of course. They'd only just barely landed on the moon. Time travel was at least several decades away. *Must be all those episodes of* The Twilight Zone *I've been tuning into lately.*

Tom had always been a fan of the uncanny and otherworldly. As a teenager, he had collected every new edition of pulp fiction like Tales from the Crypt. Eventually, his mother had forbidden him from purchasing any more, as he had begun to have nightmares induced by the gory tales within. So, it was no surprise to him that his mind had immediately turned to such fanciful theories.

Still. Something felt… wrong. Maybe even *Twilight Zone* wrong.

"Rita? Babydoll?!" No response.

Tom was getting nervous. *Where is she?* He could hear a quiet murmur coming from outside the closed door and it took only two quick steps to open it and look outside.

There was a hallway, pristine and scrupulously vacuumed. The walls were white and painted with a repeating pattern of blue waves, topped with tiny, handpainted sailboats every few feet — whoever had decorated this place obviously loved the ocean. The hardwood floors continued throughout, and soft lighting gleamed down from bulbs sunk deep into the ceiling.

Then he saw what was walking around here… and his heart began to race.

Strolling through the hallway were monsters wearing human bodies. One of them — a horrible skull with strips of flesh hanging from its jaw, sitting atop a whole and undamaged body — shuffled past him, barely glancing in his direction. It looked like it had crawled directly from the cover of a Tales from the Crypt book. Tom recoiled, biting down hard on his lip, and barely contained a scream. Pain flared in his mouth and he tasted blood.

"Rita!!" Tom was really panicking now and tears sprung to his eyes. "Rita! Where are you?!"

A body wearing beige slacks and a tan polo shirt emerged from a door across the way — its head was a slimy green snake, flicking its red tongue out as it passed. There was one in a pink dress with the hairy head and mandibles of a pitch-black spider, its eyes red and glinting in the overhead lights. It leaned down to use a water fountain, though given its lack of a tongue, Tom saw no way it could drink.

But the spider-monster's pink dress… It reminded him of something…

Rita! She had worn a sundress just that color on the night he proposed to her!

Tom stood frozen in that hallway of terrors, remembering that night, nearly fifteen years ago…

Rita's hair was chestnut-colored and shiny, cascading down her back to her waist. He had packed a picnic in a woven basket, spread a blue gingham blanket on the grass in the park near her parents' house, and she sat on it with her legs curled back, the pink sundress rippling as she moved. He loved the way it sat on her collarbone, demure and proper, but just low enough that he could see the little nubs beneath her throat. He'd made bologna and Swiss cheese sandwiches — her favorite, though he thought the cheese tasted a bit like armpits.

He watched her, grinning like a fool, as she rummaged around in the basket and pulled out a carton of strawberries. When she opened it, she gasped, shouted in delight, and threw her arms around him, tears springing to her eyes.

Inside, atop the ripe, red fruit, sat a shining diamond engagement ring.

"Think you can handle me forever, babydoll?" Tom asked her, leaning back and looking down at her grinning face.

She did, of course, and now it was fifteen years and two kids later, and they had a house and a car and a successful business. And they were happy…

Oh my god! The kids! Are they safe?! Tom was jolted from his reverie by the thought. They were just eight and ten years old, and would be terrified by these monsters!

"Rita?" he called again, softer this time. He was afraid the monsters would notice him if he made a commotion, and he didn't know what he'd do if they came at him. "Jenny? Tommy?" He hoped his children would not answer — that they were somewhere very far away.

His wife and children did not come, so Tom did the only thing he could. He picked a direction and started walking, shuddering as he passed a creature in a periwinkle-blue sleeping dress with the head of a gorgon. The snakes writhed and hissed when he glanced at it, and he quickly averted his eyes, giving it a wide berth. He'd read a comic about a gorgon once; it had depicted the monster with prominent nipples on its curvaceous, feminine body — the perfect mix of sexy and scary. Unfortunately, his mother happened to walk by while he was looking at that page one time, and had immediately grounded him for three weeks. The embarrassment had almost eclipsed the horror of the nightmares the image had caused — he'd be necking with some pretty girl from his class in some backseat of some car that wasn't his, and he'd open his eyes and find he'd been kissing a snake.

At the end of the hallway, he emerged into an open-plan room, similar to the common room in which he'd played card games with his college dormmates. Instead of students, there were more monsters with human bodies: over by the window was a mummy, dozing, half-unwrapped bandages flapping in the slight breeze; a giant fly with multi-faceted eyes looked up from the puzzle it was building and tracked Tom's progress across the room; a man reading a paperback in a large, soft armchair — navy blue stripes like the one Tom woke up in — looked normal, until Tom saw the other side of his head. It was smashed in and bloody, the brain matter exposed to the air. All of them could have walked right off the pages of those old horror comics, or the screens of trashy B-flicks that he'd seen with his friends.

Tom felt bile rising in his throat and swallowed hard, fighting the urge to gag.

One of the monsters was walking directly toward him. It wore lavender-colored hospital scrubs. Its head was a horrendous green alien with one bulging black eye. The eye, which reflected no light, pointed right at him and moved wetly in its socket as the creature spoke.

"Mister Kirkman? Is everything alright?" The eye blinked once, slowly.

Tom stumbled back a step. "What… How… How do you know my name? Where am I?"

The alien head tilted, seeming almost… sympathetic. "You're feeling a little strange, aren't you? A little confused?"

Well, that's an understatement! "More than a little!"

"How about we go back to your room? I'll help you lie down." The creature's voice was sweet and gentle, a total mismatch with her horrid appearance.

Tom was scared, and he was becoming irritated. "That wasn't my bedroom! I want to know where I am, what all these… things are, and where my wife is! I need my wife!" His voice broke and he felt ashamed at the display of emotion. This wasn't like him at all.

"I need Rita," he whispered, his voice hoarse.

The alien stepped forward and put a gentle hand on his forearm. "I understand, Mister Kirkman," it said. "You often get scared these days."

"What does that mean?" Tom snapped at her as he flinched away. He heard buzzing in his head.

No, not in his head! Another scrub-attired beast was approaching, its head a beehive, crawling with fuzzy, buzzing honeybees. Tom was afraid of bees, had been since he was stung on the armpit when he was six.

"Mister Kirkman, you have a visitor," said the beehive, the cheery voice emanating from an opening in the papery grey material, and bees flew in and out of the opening as it spoke.

Tom was horrified. He took several steps back, getting ready to turn and run. He didn't know where he would run to, just that he needed to get away.

Then he saw her.

Beside the beehive was a girl. She had long, chestnut hair cascading down her back. She was wearing a pink sundress.

Rita?

He lurched toward her, the held-back tears finally spilling from his eyes. "Oh, thank God, Rita!" he cried, and enveloped her in his arms.

Rita stiffened for a moment, then wrapped her arms around him and squeezed.

"Hi," she said, and the sound of her sweet voice pushed away all his fear. "You okay?"

Tom pressed his face into her shoulder, tears and snot soaking into the fabric. "No, babydoll! I'm not! Where are we? Why are we surrounded by monsters?"

Rita pulled away from him and inspected his face. Her plump lips shone with fresh gloss. Her freckles sprayed across her nose just like always. He wanted to kiss every one of them.

"Let's go sit down, alright? That room with the green walls? You know it?"

"Yeah…?" *What's wrong? Why is she acting weird?*

"Great, let's go there," Rita said, and took his hand. When he looked down at their interlaced fingers, he saw she wasn't wearing her wedding ring.

"Forget your ring by the sink again, babydoll?" Tom teased. It was easy to forget being scared when he was with his Rita.

She paused before answering. "Oh, yeah. I'm always forgetting, you know," she said, but her voice wavered, and Tom glanced sideways at her. *There is definitely something weird going on.*

Rita led him down the hallway and into the room with the armchair and the hardwood floors and the olive green walls with the art he didn't recognize. Rita always calmed him. She'd never been impressed by the horror flicks he'd taken her to see when he was courting her. It all looks so fake, she'd say with a laugh. And Tom would laugh along with her, the gore and screams and gruesome monsters overshadowed by her light and laughter; by her tiny hand in his; by salty, buttered popcorn on his tongue.

The creature with the alien head followed them in, and Tom raised an eyebrow, wondering what she was doing. *Doesn't she know this is a private moment with my wife?*

Rita patted his hand. "It's alright," she said. "She's just here to help you relax a bit. You haven't been sleeping enough… honey." Her voice faltered on the last word.

Tom let Rita lead him to the bed, its covers smooth and clean. She pulled back the comforter and patted the mattress. Tom started to protest, not wanting to dirty the bed with his street clothes, when he looked down and noticed for the first time that he was wearing pajamas.

"You'll just take a little nap," Rita said, holding his hand while he lay down. She pulled the blanket up and tucked it in around his chest. "You'll feel a lot better after."

Tom felt a twinge in his left arm and flinched, but before he could turn to see what it was, he noticed Rita's eyes — glossy and shimmering.

"Rita? Babydoll? You okay?" He reached his hand to wipe an escaped tear from her cheek.

Rita nodded and swallowed. She took a deep breath and smiled down at him. "I'm okay."

Tom began to feel heavy, but it did not scare him. The bed felt like a cloud, and he thought he might sleep for days.

"You'll be here when I wake up, babydoll?" he asked, his vision blurring.

"I will. I love you," she said. She leaned down and kissed him on the forehead.

He was asleep before he could respond.

"He hasn't slept in almost twenty-four hours," the nurse said. "I thought he might let us near him with the meds if you were here to calm him down."

"That was a good idea," Jenny said, nodding.

She looked down at her father's peaceful face. He was already snoring.

Jenny finished tucking the covers under his chin, then noticed the photo frame fallen over on the nightstand. She set it upright, smiling at the image and stroking it with a loving finger. Her mother, in her favorite pink sundress, smiled back at her from a moment made eternal, nearly fifty years before.

Rita would, indeed, be there when Tom woke up.

She leaned down one last time and kissed her father's papery, wrinkled cheek.

"Sleep well, Dad," she whispered, and left the room, closing the door with a quiet *click* behind her.

For my dad

HEAD TRAUMA AND A BIG PROBLEM

My writing partner, Saige, and I love to do flash exercises— it's how I got these giant muscles. This was one of the first we tried. We chose a prompt and both created a piece from it. Originally, I didn't think this piece was worthy of much more regard than a quick read on the blog, but my mom let me know when it went live that she loved it— she even said she cheered at the end. You know what I always say— the point of art is to make us feel something. Given that it spurred a response in her, I included it in this collection. Just in case it spurs a response in you, too.

The floor tasted like piss and blood.

My body was like cracked concrete where it lay against the linoleum. Hot bands of burning pain stretched across my nose, forehead, and cheek. I bit back a scream of agony as I rolled myself off my face and onto my side, groaning and willing my eyelids to peel open.

I saw the room on its side, the metal table and tools on the wall hooks still in their place just past the bars of the metal cage.

What happened? The last thing I remembered was the feeling like a train hit me in the skull.

I lifted my hand and felt around for wounds. An angry throbbing gash spread from my ear to the center back of my head. My hand came back tacky with drying blood.

How long was I out?

I felt a sense of panic begin to build, but I didn't know why. Just that I was missing something.

Bracing myself on my elbow, I heaved my battered body up to a sitting position. The motion made my head swim sickeningly, and before I knew it, I was vomiting into my lap.

The room still spun, but after blinking a few times and taking several deep breaths of sour stinking air, I felt okay enough to look around the room.

There were the bars of the cold metal cage. The bucket in the corner, now knocked on its side, a spray of cloudy piss splattered across the floor.

Of course, I stopped smelling the bucket a long time ago.

The steel surface of the examination table shined in the light of the single naked bulb hanging out of the ceiling, the plaster cracking around it. There was some blood on the table, but it looked like it was almost dry.

This caused my panic to take a stronger hold of me, though I couldn't bring to mind exactly why.

I focused on my body, what hurt and what didn't; though honestly, most of it hurt, and bad. My nose was smashed crooked and the right side of my face would be a hideous blue bruise tomorrow. There were a few long but shallow scratches on my right forearm, just deep enough for little scabs of drying blood to poke through the skin.

Wincing, I unsteadily pulled myself to my feet, which caused another wave of vertigo to smash into me like a wave. I threw out a hand and caught myself on the bars of the cage. My chest lifted and fell as I took several fortifying deep breaths.

"Okay," I said aloud to myself. "Okay, you're okay."

I lifted my head and looked out into the room, inspecting the wall. The tools hung on their pegs, many of them rusted and decaying from lack of proper care. The hacksaw was stained brown and broken on one end, barely usable. The screwdriver was stained black from constantly being heated by the torch, which lay waiting on a workbench against the wall below the peg rack. The forge hammer—

The forge hammer wasn't there. An empty spot stood out on the peg board like a mouth missing a tooth.

"Shit," I muttered to myself, "Shit, shit, shit."

My heart quickened, and I heard blood pounding in my ears. I whipped my head around the cage, causing my vision to flicker and my knees to buckle, but not before I saw it.

The door to the cage was hanging open.

When I came to the second time, I was leaned up against the bars. I hadn't cracked my face on the floor again, thankfully.

The cage. The door. It's open.

I repeated this in my mind as I slowly pulled myself to my feet, scrabbling at the bars for support.

I didn't want to black out again; something was wrong here. I needed to clear my head enough to put it together. Thoughts were so hard to hear through the church bells clanging against my skull. Just the pain alone made me feel like I might be sick again.

I managed a few steps out through the open cage door and past the examination table, and a cold breeze blew in, turning the tacky blood on the back of my head to ice against my throbbing skin.

Wait. A *breeze*.

Then an image flashed through my mind, and my body went cold.

The van in the parking lot, where the streetlight blinked on and off in the death throes of old fluorescents. The figure cloaked in shadow.

The screaming, the begging, the tears.

The blood.

I could see it, hear it again.

I spun around, forgetting my condition, and would've gone down again if I hadn't thrown a stabilizing hand out onto the exam table.

The door to the room was wide open.

A wordless groan vibrated in my chest as I realized I was probably much too late.

I lurched forward anyway, careful to move my neck gingerly, not wanting to lose my feet again. My toe kicked a pair of rusty pliers as I stepped toward the open door, sending them spinning across the filthy linoleum.

"Shit, shit, shit!" I grunted through gritted teeth.

Emerging through the door and into the chill of the deepest part of night, I looked around wildly, cursing.

Aside from a few drops of blood leading out toward the treeline and a scrap of torn blouse hanging from a bush, there was no sign of her.

Incensed, seeing nothing but blood red rage, I screamed out into the night, the echoes of my enraged cry dampened by the rustling of leaves in the wind.

She was long gone.

Shit, shit, shit.

How had she overpowered me, managed to get the forge hammer out of my hands?

That's when I knew it was all over.

For my mom

THE SAMPLE TABLE

This is the odd one out in this collection. I know I promised you dark and strange, and while this tale is certainly unusual, it isn't the kind of strange you've seen so far. There's no horror, no gore, just antics at a Costco. It was originally written as a writing exercise with Saige, where we tried writing in each other's preferred genre. If it's not your thing, don't worry. Things get quite dark after this.

Ilia poured the protein shake with great care into tiny plastic sample cups.

She took special care not to spill a single drop on the red gingham tablecloth, which she had draped over her folding table only minutes before. The protein shake was white and bubbly with froth, and the smell that arose from the sample cups reminded Ilia of both fresh vanilla and milk that was actively spoiling.

Ilia had never understood the appeal of protein shakes. But the samples were perfect for what she had in mind.

Yanni walked briskly past the seasonal décor and clearance shelves. She was not happy to be at Costco that day.

Her powder-blue athletic leggings swished as she wove her way past a mother with four kids in tow, each brat screaming about a different perceived wrong. She gritted her teeth as a group of teenagers in paisley bandeau tops and wide-legged jeans sauntered past. They took up most of the aisle, all walking in a line, and Yanni had to push down an urge to slap the phone from the nearest girl's manicured hand.

Yanni hated going to Costco on the weekend. But Julie had forgotten to put the chicken on the counter to thaw.

So now here was Yanni on her way home from Pilates, fighting for her life past hordes of screaming children and inconsiderate teens, all for one package of fresh organic chicken breast.

Yanni loved her wife, but if her forgetfulness ended up being the reason she had to entertain her in-laws while fighting a migraine tonight, Julie would owe her a week's worth of back massages.

Yanni thought perhaps, as she stalked past the bread aisle and narrowly dodged past a worker on a pallet jack, she might be more testy than usual this morning because of her missed breakfast.

She always tried to prep for her Pilates classes with a nice protein bar. It fueled her workout and kept her from getting too peckish right afterward. Today she'd somehow forgotten to snag one on her way out after kissing Julie on the cheek. As a result, her stomach gurgled as she hurried past crackers and cookies and cake batter boxes.

So, when she saw the sample table, it was like an answered prayer.

All thoughts of the chicken, her exhausting in-laws, and her irritation with Julie vanished as Yanni saw the gorgeous young worker standing there with a table stacked full of tiny plastic cups filled with liquid protein. The woman had doll-like freckles and angular brows and a nose like a button. She looked almost like a little pixie.

Yanni's grimace of irritation melted as she approached the table, and the cute worker returned her smile right back.

She saw the woman's amber eyes dart down and to the side, and Yanni knew she was checking out her muscles and tattoos.

You're lucky I'm married, girlie, Yanni thought, and wondered what Julie would think of this little garden sprite of a catch. They loved pointing out beautiful women to each other while in public; it was a game for them.

"Hello," the freckled woman said. "Can I offer you a sample? It's a new recipe."

Yanni grinned. "You know, I'd love one. Missed my breakfast this morning, and I've got a stressful day ahead."

The woman's eyes flicked over her biceps again. "Just came from the gym?"

"Pilates, yeah."

The woman's face brightened as she smiled even wider. "I bet you have really strong shoulders!"

Yanni laughed, then grabbed one of the tiny plastic cups of frothy shake. She gulped the small portion down eagerly, and was trying to formulate a negatory response if this woman continued to put moves on her when the Costco spun around her. There was a bright blue light, then nothing.

One down, Ilia thought excitedly. *And those* shoulders*! She'll be perfect.* She glanced around to make sure none of the chaotic shoppers had seen the athletic woman disappear in a bright blue flash. Nobody was paying her any mind.

She began to wait again.

Rod could not find his wife.

They'd been together when they walked in, that much he was sure of. And they'd been together at the bread aisle, but by the time Rod was surrounded by pallets of canned chili, she was nowhere in sight.

She did this to him often. Something would catch her eye, and she would wander off without a word. Rod would constantly find himself asking her about a product or their grocery list, only to be met with silence. He would then spin around and find her fifty feet away, feeling a pair of fuzzy socks between her fingers, or examining a display of discounted wines.

He often called his wife his little squirrel, and it wasn't just because she was cute and small.

"Keisha?" He called out, and was only rewarded with an irritated glance from a middle-aged woman in beige leggings that jumpscared him into thinking she was walking around pantsless.

Rod sighed and resigned himself to their old game. He would walk to the end of his aisle, then slowly pace back and forth, looking down each one for his wife. Once, he'd completed a search of every grocery aisle in a Walmart before giving up and calling her cell phone, and she'd explained that she'd been in the chips aisle the whole time. The aisle from which he'd started.

"Keisha, baby?" He tried again, raising his voice a bit louder.

His wife did not appear around the corner, so he strode down the aisle.

But when he emerged out the other end, something caught his eye.

An adorable little freckled woman giving away samples at a cheery folding table. Little cups of white liquid dotted the gingham cloth, and Rod saw display bottles of a protein shake brand he'd never heard of before.

The displayed price per bottle was three dollars cheaper than the brand he'd been drinking for two years.

She'll just have to find me *this time*, Rod thought, and approached the table.

"Hello, sir. Can I offer you a sample? It's a new recipe," the woman said with a cheery smile.

Rod reached for a tiny cup, the cords in his strong forearms twitching with the motion. "Sure. This stuff is way cheap!"

"Are you a bodybuilder?" The woman asked, gesturing to his muscles, visible clearly despite his loose black T-shirt.

Rod chuckled. "Pretty easy to tell, huh?"

The woman only smiled as he sipped the vanilla-flavored liquid, some of it splashing up and wetting his philtrum.

Then Rod saw a flash of blue light, and the Costco faded to black.

One more and I should have enough, Ilia thought as she gave a cursory wave at a toddler who was openly staring in her direction. The toddler tugged on his mother's hand and pointed, but the woman ignored him, continuing her conversation on her cell phone.

I love those little rectangles, Ilia thought with a smile. *Always keeping them distracted.*

Benny wanted to look at the toy section. There were so many things in there— trucks, Barbies, dinosaurs, plushies— and Benny's mamá always let him pick one out when they went to Costco. He wasn't ready to start begging quite yet, but if his mamá started leading him toward the checkout line without taking him to pick out a toy, he was ready to start screaming.

Benny was ruminating on this, as much as his three-year-old mind could ruminate, when the lady caught his eye.

She had a kind smile like his babysitter, Señorita Isabel. Her round cheeks were dotted with freckles, and her facial features reminded Benny of his favorite doll, an orange-haired fairy named Poppy. The woman waved at him, smiling. He liked her. He wanted to go say hi.

Benny tugged on his mamá's hand and pointed, but she continued to talk faster than he could follow on her cell phone. Benny liked her cell phone; she let him play games on it sometimes. But other times, she ignored him and only talked to the cell phone instead of him.

"Mamá," Benny said, pulling on her hand.

"Un momento, mi hijo," his mamá replied quickly before continuing her constant stream of chatter.

Benny felt his eyes water with frustration, and was considering a good, cathartic cry until his mamá began to guide him in the direction of the freckled lady, albeit in a distracted manner.

Benny stared at the freckled lady as they made their slow way in her direction. They stopped so his mamá could inspect a box of Reddi-Rice before placing it back on the shelf, still chattering into her phone almost without pausing for breath.

The next time he looked, a woman in pink shorts with big muscles was talking to the freckled lady. His big brown eyes watched as the pink-shorts lady reached out a hand for one of the little cups of white stuff, then cry out with surprise as she knocked over several of the cups, apologizing profusely.

The freckled lady smiled and consoled the woman as the white liquid from the spilled cups began to drop down the side of the little folding table, making a small puddle on the floor.

Then the pink shorts lady reached out again and took a sample cup, upending its contents into her mouth.

Benny watched with the believing eyes of a toddler as the pink shorts lady disappeared in a flash of blue.

Then the freckled lady smiled and snapped her fingers, and she too was lost in the same blue light, and this time, the entire sample table disappeared with her.

Benny's mamá let go of his little hand briefly to grab for a jar of peanut butter off the shelf, her other hand still supporting her phone against her ear.

He took the opportunity to sneak away then, taking his unsteady, stumpy-legged steps toward the spot where the table had been. The puddle of white goo was still coagulating on the tiled floor.

Yanni blinked slowly as the world came back into focus.

Her eyes burned from the flash of light. Her first thought upon awakening was that she was sure to end up with that migraine now.

As her vision adjusted, she realized she was still standing.

And found that she was in a cage.

The bars were not metal or wood, but a glowing blue light, the same shade of the one she'd seen just before she—

Before she what, exactly? Teleported?

Yanni looked past the glowing blue bars and found that she was imprisoned in the center of a living room. She was instantly reminded of Julie's cottagecore Pinterest boards. Vines and potted plants of all shapes and colors took up every surface in the room, hanging from wall shelves and lining windowsills. The furniture was mismatched in a purposeful sort of way, the cushions of the couch well-worn but scrupulously clean, the wood of the tiny round table and two chairs were shiny with age but clean of any stains or scrapes. There was a faint smell of flowers and baked goods in the air. She heard no voices, saw no other people.

The hell? Yanni thought.

She expected to be injured in some way, bruised, shackled, even her hair to be mussed. But she couldn't find anything amiss, aside from the creeping onset of a headache, but she attributed that to the lingering effects of the Costco.

Next she inspected the inside of her cage. She had enough room to sit down, but not much more than that. The spaces between bars looked to be about six inches. The carpet beneath her was the shaggy orange type that reminded her of her grandmother's house.

What exactly are these? She wondered, inspecting the blue bars of light. Wary, she pulled off her sneaker and reached out with it slowly. When the sneaker touched the bar, it vibrated in an instantly awful way, almost exactly like touching an electric fence, which she'd done on several occasions at her childhood friend's ranch.

She cried out at the sensation and, in her surprise, the sneaker flew from her hand. It went through the bars, fell down to the carpet and bounced twice before coming to rest some three feet from the cage.

Yanni stared at it. *Great. Whatever's going on here, I'm going to face it with one shoe.*

That was when she resolved to sit quietly and wait for…

For whoever brought me here, I guess, she thought, and sat down with her legs crossed.

Yanni didn't have to wait long for something to happen.

In a familiar flash, there was suddenly another cage, identical to hers, a few feet away from her in the strange but cozy cottage. Once her vision adjusted from the light, she realized she could hear yelling.

It was coming from the new cage's occupant. He was a massive Black man, bulging with the muscles of a dedicated heavy lifter. He stopped yelling, rubbed his eyes, then spun around wildly.

"What the… Hello? *Hello?*" he cried, then his eyes fell on Yanni in her cage.

Yanni looked at him. "Uh. Hey."

"What is this? Where are we?"

"Don't know either of those," Yanni answered, "But I do know that touching those bars doesn't feel good. Don't recommend it."

So of course, the man reached out with his bare hand and yelped.

"Dude," Yanni said.

"Who.. who are you?" he asked, wringing his hand.

"I'm Yanni," she said, carefully reaching her arm out through the bars toward him, offering a hand.

The man stared at her for a few moments, distrusting, before carefully reaching a hand out toward hers, but when he reached far enough that his gargantuan upper arm touched the bars, he gave another startled cry and jerked his hand back.

"Christ," Yanni said appreciatively. "Those are huge."

The man rubbed his bicep, frowning. "I'm Rodney. Call me Rod."

"Rod. Were you… also at Costco just now?"

Rod looked at her with an eyebrow raised. "Yeah. I had…" he looked around, as if for bits of his memory, "A sample? A protein shake." He paused for a moment, then added belatedly, "It was good."

Yanni straightened. "Me too! The sample table!"

Rod's eyes were alight. "That woman... Do you think she did this?"

Yanni hesitated. "I mean, all reason points to yes, but, like, that would mean she used... magic. On us. I mean, I literally blinked and then I was here. That has to be magic, right?"

Rod thought for a moment, crossing his massive phone-book-ripping arms across his barrel chest. "I don't see why not."

Yanni exhaled and looked around the room again, not looking for anything in particular. "Alright. Okay. So we've been magically transported and imprisoned by some sort of... witch?"

"Fairy," Rod said softly, then found Yanni staring at him in confusion. He shrugged. "Her face, the freckles. I don't know. She just reminded me of a fairy." He looked down, self-conscious.

"This place does have more of a Winx Club vibe than a Hansel and Gretel witch vibe, so I guess we can call her that for now," Yanni said, rubbing at her forehead. She was feeling a bit overwhelmed at the turn of events her afternoon had taken.

There were a few moments of silence, then Rod began to chuckle, a sound like boulders rolling down a hill.

"What?" Yanni said, fighting to keep her face straight.

"It's just... My wife," he said, then the chuckles turned into belly laughs. "I always lose her in the store, and this time, she lost *me*!"

Then Yanni was laughing too. The situation was too absurd not to.

A third flash of blue light cut their laughter short. Another cage flashed into existence beside Rod's, and Yanni had to lean and peer between the bars of the two cages to see another woman, shorter than her, wearing pink biker shorts and whimpering.

"How many can fit in here?" Yanni wondered aloud. The cottage was spacious, but not giant.

"Hey," Rod said, holding a hand up. "It's alright. You're not hurt," he said to the newcomer, who looked at him and stumbled back a step, causing her to touch her back to the light bars, and she screamed.

"Shit," Rod said, turning to Yanni. "Sometimes I forget I can be... intimidating."

Yanni raised her voice for the woman to hear her over her screaming. "Hey! It's okay! We're trapped just like you!"

The woman in the pink shorts looked around and saw Yanni. She closed her mouth and returned to her whimpering, which Yanni appreciated heartily, given her incoming headache.

"Where—" she began, but was cut off as a brilliant flash of blue light tore through the center of the cottage.

When it faded, Yanni could see the freckled sample girl, standing free and smiling.

"Great! We're all here," the girl said, and clasped her hands before her in excitement.

"Now," Ilia said, standing there, still in her Costco worker uniform, "You're probably all a little confused."

All three of her captured mortals began talking at once, and she put up her hands. They quieted.

"I haven't brought you here to hurt you, and I give you my word that if you do as I request, you will be returned to where I stole you from."

"Why should we believe that?" the man asked in a strong voice.

Ilia gave him a flat look. "Um. I'm Fae. I literally can't lie."

"What is this?" the pink shorts girl whimpered, tears in her eyes.

"Hey, you don't gotta do that," Ilia said, snapping her fingers. She released the magic on all of the cage bars and the room dimmed considerably without their glow. "It's alright, see? I give you my word, I won't hurt you."

The pink shorts girl started for the front door, a beautiful oak piece inset with stained glass. It had been a gift from Ilia's mother. She raised a hand, and the edges of the door glowed blue.

"Sorry, can't let you do that," she said with regret. "Mortals really shouldn't go out in the Fae realm without supervision. It can really mess you up. Your mind, I mean. Well, I guess there are the

Fae beasts and they really like the taste of mortal flesh, but can you really blame them?"

Ilia stopped as she realized her captives were staring at her with wide, frightened eyes. The pink shorts girl continued to cry.

"Sorry, sorry, that's not- I just- Okay, look. I brought you all here because I need help," Ilia said in her most disarming voice.

The blue-leggings woman and the muscled man exchanged a glance.

"Our help?" The man said.

"Yeah. Here, take a seat," Ilia said, gesturing to the couch and stuffed chairs surrounding her oak coffee table, which overflowed with plants and ceramics she'd fired herself.

The blue-leggings woman was the first to move. First, she walked over and picked up her missing shoe. Then she made her slow way to the floral-patterned armchair and lowered herself gently, as if expecting it to blow up. It didn't. She put her shoe on and got to work tying the laces.

Her safe arrival into a seat spurned the other two to join her, though Pink Shorts was still sniffling.

Ilia smiled and snapped.

Nothing happened.

She frowned, then groaned.

"Damn, I keep forgetting," she said to herself, then looked out at her seated mortals. "So sorry there's no tea. It's kind of part of my problem I need help with. You, Pink Shorts. You can stop crying now, please."

Pink Shorts looked up with wet eyes. "My name isn't Pink Shorts. It's-"

"*Don't!*" the man cried, springing to his feet.

Both mortals looked at him.

"Haven't you read a book before?" the man said, shaken. "You *never* give a Fae your name. They have power over you if you do."

Ilia smiled. "At least one of you beefheads has a brain. He's right, Pink Shorts. That's why I didn't ask for it. Sign of goodwill."

Pink Shorts looked stunned, then finally appeared to relax some.

"Okay, wow, this has really gotten away from me," Ilia started. "Okay. I brought you all here using my protein shake—"

"*That's* how you did it!" the man cried again, still on his feet. "Never accept food from a Fae. They can use it to transport you to the Fae realm."

"Dude, where did you learn this stuff?" Blue Leggings asked.

"Audiobooks," the man said gruffly. "Got a problem?"

"Hey, no judgment," she said. "Just surprised."

"Hey, guys?" Ilia said, waving a hand to get their attention. "I was kind of talking."

"I'm sorry," the man said. "Just got a little excited." He sat back down.

Ilia exhaled. She was regretting so many things at that moment.

"Okay. As I was saying, I brought you all here using the protein shake. I thought it would lure people who work out, you know? Athletic people, like you guys. See, I've recently-"

Everyone jumped, including Ilia, as another flash of blue light blinded them all.

When it faded and their retinas adjusted, Ilia groaned.

"What the *hell*?" the man said.

"Oh, you've got to be kidding," Ilia said, throwing a hand over her eyes in exasperation.

A toddler stood in a blue-light cage in the middle of her cottage, looking around with wide brown eyes. There was sticky protein shake smeared across his chin and nose.

He looked around. His lip began to quiver.

"For fuck's sake," Ilia said and snapped her fingers. The cage bars disappeared.

The toddler made an uncertain noise that indicated he was well on his way to a full-on bawl. Then his eyes landed on Ilia, and his face melted into recognition.

He stumbled toward her on stubby legs, babbling, "Fairy!"

Ilia looked to her mortals for help as the child extended his arms up to her, giggling.

"How did—" the man began.

"I spilled some," Pink Shorts said in a quiet, thick voice. "When I knocked those cups over. He must've eaten it off the floor."

"Oh, gross," Blue Leggings said, gagging. "Only a toddler would eat off the floor of a *Costco*."

"This is *not* ideal," Ilia said hopelessly and sighed heavily. "We've got to get rid of him or we'll never get this done."

"Get *rid* of him?" Blue leggings repeated with horror.

"Whoa, not like that," Ilia said, insulted. She went into the kitchen, the child trailing behind her like a cat. She pulled a cloth off the top of the big wooden bowl that had been left on the counter. Inside was a thick goo tinged a corpselike blue color. It smelled like vanilla and honey.

Ilia opened a drawer and reached for a spoon, but it wouldn't move when she curled her fingers around the handle and lifted.

"*Arggh*," Ilia growled, then whirled around and stomped back to the living room, where her captives watched with big eyes.

"One of you, come here please."

Nobody moved.

"For shit's sake, I just need one of you to lift this spoon!"

Blue Leggings decided to be brave, apparently. She followed Ilia into the tiny, cramped kitchen.

"Just any of those, please," Ilia said, rubbing circles on her temples.

Blue Leggings took a spoon from the open drawer, hesitant, as if expecting something momentous.

"Great," Ilia said. She pointed at the toddler clinging to her leg. "Now feed him some of *that*," she said, gesturing to the wooden bowl of blue sludge.

"I'm not sure how comfortable I am feeding a baby some random goo that's been sitting out for who knows how long," Blue Leggings said, gesturing with the spoon.

Ilia was losing her grip on her patience and her sanity. She exhaled and forced her voice to stay steady.

"I give my word that the 'random goo' will do nothing to the kid aside from send him right back to where he disappeared," Ilia said.

Blue Leggings looked at her for a moment, then nodded. "Okay."

She scooped a generous serving of the goo out of the bowl and lowered the spoon down to the child, who turned his head away and hid behind Ilia's leg.

"Oh, it's gonna be like this, is it?" Blue Leggings said. She looked at Ilia. "This is why I'm not having kids."

What commenced was a chaotic and horrendously loud chase through Ilia's kitchen and the rest of the cottage as Blue Leggings tried to get any amount of the goo into the child's mouth. He evaded with expert skill, taking down plant pots and tapestries in his path. When the situation began to feel hopeless, the man stood and attempted to herd the child toward Blue Leggings, which earned him a hearty smack directly in the groin. He crumpled to the floor as the toddler zoomed away, laughing and knocking over Ilia's white orchids and spilling dark potting soil across her wooden floor.

Finally, the issue was resolved by Pink Shorts, who helpfully suggested that they simply leave a puddle of the blue goo on the floor and pretend the child didn't exist. "It worked with the protein shake," she said, and none of them could think of a better solution, so onto the floor it went.

Two minutes later, Ilia's shoulders slumped with relief as the toddler winked out of her realm. She simply sat for a moment, regretting every line of thought that had led to this decision.

"Um, I'm getting kind of hungry," Blue Leggings said, and Ilia looked at her.

Ilia sighed. "My boyfriend and I broke up a few days ago. He was kind of a dick about it. He enchanted all my furniture so that I, or any other Fae, can't move it while it's in my house." She gestured vaguely around the cottage. "It's why I needed you to move that spoon. I can't move anything in here unless it's not in the house, but I obviously can't take it out of the house."

"That's… Wow," Blue Leggings said. "Pretty diabolical, really. Can you like, get under the covers in bed at least?"

Ilia shook her head. "Nope. That's why I lured you all with a protein shake. I needed strong, athletic mortals to help me move all my stuff out of here."

The man spoke. "That's why you kidnapped us? You need help *moving*?"

Ilia puffed up her chest. "Yep. Pretty proud of the whole thing, really. I bet Lucian didn't think I'd be able to sort this crap out so soon. That asshole."

"Wait," the man said, "if you can't even pick up your spoons, how'd you make the protein shake and..." He glanced at the coagulating blue goo on the floor. "*That*?"

Ilia smiled. "I bought it. I have a friend who does custom concoctions."

"So," Pink Shorts said, "You need us to move all your stuff out of here. Where are we going to put it after that?"

"Oh, I can handle all that stuff once it's outside," Ilia said with a dismissive wave. "I've got a new place lined up, and I'll just winnow it over there."

"This is the weirdest day of my life," the man said with a far-away look in his eyes.

"Still better than cooking for my in-laws," Blue Leggings said. "Speaking of, when we get back to Costco, can you guys remind me to pick up some chicken?"

"So everyone's good?" Ilia said, beginning to bounce excitedly on her heels.

The man shrugged. "Sure. Should be easy."

"Yeah, I've helped a ton of friends move," Blue Leggings said. "But they usually give me pizza when we're done."

Pink Shorts nodded. "I'll do it for pizza."

"Mortals are fascinating," Ilia said quietly.

"Dude, this is some alternate Fae world," Blue Leggings said, rolling her eyes. "What makes you think they have *pizza*?"

"Aww, man," the man said, sagging. "Now I want pizza."

Ilia looked at them. "We have pizza."

"What?" the man said.

"Of course we have pizza," Ilia said. "It's like, the best mortal invention of all time."

Later, Ilia sat in her new living room, her furniture and plants (the ones that survived the toddler) already in place. By winnowing the furniture, she was able to instantly place everything in its right place with a snap of her fingers once it was outside her old cottage.

Blue Leggings, the man, and Pink Shorts sat around her, sweating and fanning themselves with their hands. It had been hard work, but none of them had complained. They seemed to revel in the physical labor.

Ilia thought it was simply fascinating. She vowed to herself to try to spend more time around mortals after this. They were just so interesting.

Then, as promised, she snapped her fingers, and two steaming hot, greasy, cheesy pizzas appeared on the coffee table before them. They all dug in eagerly.

Yanni unlocked her front door and pushed it open. She wanted to get in the shower immediately; between Pilates and her afternoon activities, she reeked of sweat.

She walked inside the apartment, and then Julie was there, kissing her on the cheek and squeezing her shoulder.

"Hey babe," Julie said, stepping back to look at her wife. "Wow, tough Pilates class today? You're sweaty," she said, teasing.

"You don't know the half of it," Yanni said. "I need a shower, pronto."

Julie looked at Yanni again, her face confused. "I thought you were stopping by Costco. Where's the chicken?"

Yanni stared at her wife, then said, "*Shit.*"

For Saige, of course

BRICKS

It's often said that Stephen King can't write endings. While I strongly disagree, I do understand how some might see a few of his as open-ended. I think people really tend to miss the point of stories with open endings. Either that, or I'm just bad at endings. I'll let you decide. After reading it, my dad pointed out that it's actually a really good metaphor for the struggle with mental illness and the obstacles it can put in the way of daily living. Perhaps you'll agree with him, or you'll be mad at me about that whole ending thing. It was originally published in the October 2025 issue of Tumbleweird, and I again have Lari to thank for the excellent editing- this story had some SERIOUS issues before they got their genius hands on it.

The day the first brick appeared, I was at work, typing vendor data into an Excel sheet. I was twenty-two years old and things were still mostly alright, I thought. I'd quit the stress eating, moved past the unbearable weight of my inferiority, my life, the heavy expectations I placed on myself — my psychiatrist had helped me realize these stressors were self-perpetuating. My boss, Jared, was a really nice guy — laid back, gave me time off whenever I wanted it. I liked him. Even now, he texts me occasionally to ask how I'm doing and invites me out for a drink. I've stopped responding, though — I wouldn't even know what to say.

On that first, fateful day, I hit 'Enter' and the spreadsheet auto-formatted a number for the tenth time. *Ugh! Spreadsheets! I need to eat something.*

The brick was one of those things that you don't notice immediately, like a new eye floater. As I rifled through my snack drawer, looking for a granola bar to quell my irritation, something on the floor caught my eye.

I closed the drawer and looked at it. *What…?* I rubbed my eyes, opened them again. It was still there: just a brick, nothing special — it was that reddish color like the ones my grandma's house is made of. I reached to grab it and my fingers gripped its sharp edges, but I couldn't pry it off the ground.

"The fuck?" I said, tapping my foot tentatively against the brick.

Kendra, at her desk in the next cubicle, was peering into a hand mirror and reapplying her mascara. She grunted something unintelligible. She was my best friend at work, the only one who had sent me a card when I had a meltdown last year and spent three days in the crisis ward.

"Where did this come from?" I asked her.

"Huh?"

"There's a… a brick here."

I scooted my chair away from the desk, trying to get a better angle. *Maybe if I stand I can get more leverage to pick it up.* But as my chair rolled backwards, my stomach lurched. The brick moved with me, sliding silently across the floor and remaining fixed slightly to my left and a couple feet away.

"Kendra?" My voice shook. "Come here for a minute."

She rose from behind the partition, heaving a sigh, her chair wheels squealing. When she walked around her desk and stopped in front of me, her foot was inches from the brick. She looked at me, a hand on her hip and one eyebrow raised.

"Doll, your face is white as my ass in December. You okay?"

"It's…" I pointed at the brick. "I can't… it's stuck there."

"What is, doll?"

"That brick." *What does she mean? It's right there!*

Kendra looked at where I pointed, looked back at me, her brow furrowing. "The floor's carpet, doll."

Why is she messing with me?! "Kendra! The brick! On the floor! Right there by your foot!"

Kendra looked down — right at the brick.

"I don't… Are you…? Should I get some help?" Her eyes softened and her voice did that thing people do when they're trying to soothe a fussing child.

"Ugh! Here!" I reached to grab her wrist and pulled her hand to the brick, but where it should have made contact, it just… disappeared. Inside the brick. My hand slammed into it, its coarse surface scratching my palm.

I recoiled with a sharp exhale and rolled backwards again. Again, the brick moved with me, staying the same distance from me, in the same position.

"The fuck?!" I shouted. *What is happening?!*

"Kat, what's...?"

I leapt from my chair and stepped back several steps, my butt slamming into another desk behind me. The brick followed. I slid along the edge of the desk, exiting the cubicle sideways. The brick stayed with me — solid, silent, spooky as hell. I started to cry.

As I stared at the brick, dread filled my chest and I struggled to breathe. It represented all the things I thought I had overcome — the things I'd been told were all in my head, made up by my own brain.

Jared poked his head out of his office. "Everything okay?"

"I... The... Excuse me!" I stumbled out of my cube and ran for the bathroom, slamming the door shut behind me and snapping the lock closed — *surely it can't follow me in here!* My reflection in the large mirror on the back of the door showed my eyes wide and white, my hair half fallen out of its banana clip. My heart was beating too fast and my legs were shaking. I felt like I might fall over.

Oh heck, I need to pee! As I turned away from the door and stepped towards the toilet, I froze. The brick was inside the bathroom. My bladder cramped and I got my pants off as fast as I could, relief flooding through me when I sat down and released the flow, even as my brain was screaming at me to *Run!*

I never took my eyes off it as I urinated, expecting it to strike at any moment, like a predator in stealth mode. I stared so hard my eyes started burning. I stood up, flushed without turning my head. I went to the sink and washed my hands — and watched as it moved with me, never deviating from its position.

As I walked back to my desk, I watched the brick sliding over the blue rayon carpet. I passed someone in the corridor carrying a stack of papers, their foot on a direct collision course with the brick. I half-opened my mouth to warn them and cringed as their foot collided with it, expecting them and their papers to go flying.

Instead, their foot flickered and vanished for an instant, passing through the brick without even a hitch in their step. *Huh?!*

Suddenly, the noise in the office was very loud. The lights buzzed. Everything felt kind of blurry at the edges — a grey mist creeping over my vision. I reached my desk and groped for my chair, sitting down hard and gripping the armrests so tightly my knuckles turned white.

"Kat? Is everything okay?" The calm, measured voice emerged from the maelstrom. *Jared.* I looked up and shook my head slightly to clear my vision. He and Kendra stood at the entrance to my cube, looking at me like I was a bomb about to explode.

"I, uh…" I glanced down at the brick. *No. Nothing about this is okay.* I rolled my chair forward and the brick travelled with me, clipping through a trash can and reappearing on the other side like a poorly rendered video game object. It was too much for me. *Get out! Get out! Can't breathe!*

"My… my aunt died," I sputtered — the first excuse I thought of. "I need to go."

I sat at home for two days, and the brick sat with me. Always on my left. Always two feet away.

Human brains can get used to pretty much anything, and once I got over the initial shock, I began thinking of it as nothing more than an interesting anomaly. After all, Aunt Nicki swore up and down she could see a man behind her in the guest bathroom mirror; a man who wasn't there when she turned around. It scared the shit out of her the first time, but she said he never did anything, just stood there.

"Our brains are really just computers," she would always say — the story was her go-to at family gatherings. "Sometimes they short-circuit."

I figured that if someone as put-together as Aunt Nicki can see shit like that, I was fine. Apparently, my brain short-circuited and created an imaginary brick companion. I could accept that.

It definitely was *not* related to my meltdown the year before! Like, sure, I get stressed sometimes to the point of breaking, but nothing is *actually* wrong with me. I come from a decent family, was never abused, never experienced any *real* trauma. Nothing was wrong enough to make me truly delusional. This was just a blip, a brain glitch, a harmless man behind me in the mirror.

That line of thinking worked for six months. Then the second brick appeared.

It was at my twenty-third birthday dinner. My second margarita had sent me weaving for the bathroom, and I saw a new brick on the floor, moving perfectly in time with my unsteady steps. I stumbled to a stop and looked back at my family digging into their enchilada platters and beef burritos, but of course nobody else had noticed it.

"Kat?" my mom mumbled through a mouthful of rice. "You good?"

I knew she thought I was sloshed — two empty oversized margarita glasses sat in front of my half-eaten plate, only a bit of ice left melting at the bottom.

"Yeah, yeah. Just… gotta pee," I stammered, and beelined for the ladies'.

I sat on the toilet and stared at the new brick, the moment mirrored from six months before. This time, Mariachi music played through speakers above the door and the smell of fresh tortillas mingled with the lavender bathroom perfume.

The new brick was about a foot to the right of the first brick — same color, same size. I could reach out and feel its rough surface, but I could not pick it up. It moved with me, always holding its position and distance.

By the time I returned to the table, I had my breathing under control, but I was shaking and lightheaded through the rest of the meal. My sisters teased me about overdoing it on the margaritas. For once, I didn't defend myself. I laughed with them. I ate the rest of my food. I watched the bricks from the corner of my eye, and said nothing. I'd rather they think I was a raging alcoholic than insane.

The real panic began when the third brick appeared while I was grocery shopping three months later. Then the fourth and fifth only two days after that. In six months, I was up to twenty-five. They seemed to appear faster the more I thought about them, like a horror movie where just *thinking* about the ghost will bring it to you. I finally understood the depths of the horror that awaited me: the bricks would keep coming, in higher numbers every time, and I didn't know if they would stop before they walled me in.

I tried everything. I bought a plane ticket to Europe when I turned twenty-five, thinking maybe they couldn't follow me into the air, couldn't travel across that much water. The flight attendant's polished black pumps just flickered through the wall of bricks as if they were a mirage.

I've tried smashing the bricks with hammers and picks. Every tool passed straight through them — the first time I tried landed me in the hospital with a busted kneecap, the momentum of my strike carrying the hammer straight through the brick and into me.

I bought a solvent that said it would dissolve mortar. It slopped off the head of the applicator and spilled through the bricks, pooling on the floor and permanently staining my living room carpet.

Nothing could touch the bricks, but they weren't intangible. Not, at least, for me.

I got weird looks at checkout counters when I insisted on standing at a certain angle relative to the employee helping me, so I started telling people I was losing my sight. How else could I explain that I could only see things if they were in a very particular spot on my right? It wasn't a lie. Not really. The bricks had blocked about two-thirds of my field of vision.

I tried for a long time to keep working. I couldn't drive anymore — I took Ubers, carpooled, even begged my sisters for rides. In the end, my unraveling mental state pulled the plug for me.

Jared was so patient, so understanding. After I had failed to escape the bricks via plane, I sat down on the filthy airport floor and called his cell, sobbing uncontrollably. I hadn't really been thinking, just pressed 'call' on the first name I saw in my recents. I was awfully embarrassed after, but he assured me that he was here for me, even just as a listening ear. I don't know how I got so lucky. If I'd worked anywhere else, I would've been called in by HR the next day, I know it.

Part of me thinks there could have been something between us, if I hadn't been so preoccupied with the bricks. He was unmarried, as far as I knew — never wore a ring, anyway. I liked the way he dressed and his soft smile. I have no idea if he ever thought of me that way, but I never asked. There had been that one time, when I went to deliver some reports, and he'd caught my hand gently, making me gasp.

"Your hands!" he said. "What happened?"

I didn't know how to explain that the scrapes and scars were from accidentally smashing my hands on the bricks, so I shrugged it off with some half-assed story about a home DIY project.

That was a year ago.

Kendra was gone — giving birth to her third kid had finally convinced her to stay home with them. At her going away party, I'd smashed my knuckles on the bricks *again*, trying to catch a lighter someone tossed at me to light the candles on her cake. Old reactions die hard, I guess.

My new cube-mate, Dom, was a nice enough guy, but a crappy worker. I had to pick up a lot of slack after we lost Kendra. I don't think it contributed to my breakdown — the bricks were more than enough to do that — but I bet Jared still thinks it did. I never told him the real reason I left.

I was broke, living paycheck-to-paycheck — transportation costs ate up most of my salary and the cash I got when I sold my car only lasted a few months. I knew I had my family to drive me if I really needed it, but I couldn't bother them for little things. I couldn't bring myself to beg them for rides except in emergencies, like when my aunt actually did die and we all had to drive up to Springfield for the funeral.

My last day at work started going downhill when Dom asked me to grab a box of manila folders from the supply shelf. I angled myself so I could reach through my opening. As I lifted onto my toes and thrust my hand toward the gap in the bricks, aiming for the folder box, a new brick appeared *right* at the moment my hand reached the opening.

My hand smashed into the brick and one of my fingernails bent back. It hurt like ever-loving sin, and I lost it.

"Fuck! Fucking *fuck!*" I shouted, clutching my throbbing hand to my chest. Tears stung my eyes. *This is so unfair! Why do I have to live like this?!*

"Kat?" Jared emerged from the employee kitchen with a steaming plate. It smelled like Mexican food.

"Fuck, this hurts!" I said through gritted teeth. My nail throbbed and burned, the pain building. The seconds ticked past. I could see blood welling along the sides of the nail. "Fucking *bricks!* Fuck this!"

Tears streamed down my face and I did nothing to try and stop them. I no longer cared what anyone thought of me. I was done. That *fucking* brick! Showing up right in that *fucking* moment! It just made me so. Fucking. *Mad!* I let out a shriek and, in a mad burst of energy, directed all my weight and fury into the supply shelf. The flimsy metal shelf crashed to the floor, boxes of paper and thumbtacks and sticky notes tumbling off it like rocks in an avalanche. The office chatter went silent — my colleagues turned as one to stare.

"Kat!" Jared shouted. I couldn't see him. My heartbeat sounded in my ears and my breath came fast and shallow. The pain in my finger wasn't easing. I felt more trapped by the bricks than ever before. I opened my mouth to scream again, not sure if I'd be able to stop this time.

And then, Jared was bursting through the bricks on my left, flickering through them like they were nothing. He reached out to touch my arm, his grip cool and firm. He looked at me with his eyes wide, the pupils dilated with fear and uncertainty. "Kat? Can we calm down here? What's the problem?"

And that was it. I was done. Seeing Jared look at me like that — like I was dangerous, unstable — was what broke me. Because I knew that I *was* becoming unstable.

I jerked my arm from his grip. I was crying, gasping great, heaving sobs: "I'm sorry! I tried. I tried! I can't anymore. I'm sorry."

I ran through the office and out the front door. I imagined the shocked faces of Dom, of Jared, of all my coworkers as they watched me flee. I could almost *hear* them gossiping about my dramatic departure in the breakroom later.

Things got much worse after that.

I spent twenty dollars on an Uber home and cried in the backseat for the whole ride. The driver eyed me in the rearview mirror and handed me a box of Kleenex he had on the passenger seat, then turned up the radio and left me alone. I guess they get used to that kind of thing.

I had no savings and about three hundred dollars in my checking account. I lay on the couch for a week, then two. I ate the forgotten food in my kitchen — a can of lima beans, three cans of sweet corn, pasta sauce, canned tuna, yogurt a month past expiration, hot dogs from a long-opened package. When I got down to two tiny cans of mushrooms and a jar of strawberry jelly, I realized I needed to figure out what to do.

How about just dying? No. I couldn't kill myself. I was too afraid of the pain. And anyway, I didn't want to. I wanted to figure out how to *live.*

I couldn't work anymore. Every time I thought about it, I felt my fingernail burst with pain, saw Jared look at me like a rabid animal…

I needed someone to take care of me. Without a job, moving back in with my parents wasn't an option. They had made that clear the day I turned sixteen — no freeloaders! And it's not like I could just rock up and tell them: "Hey, so I'm living inside this increasingly closed in room that is probably gonna kill me one day but you can't see it and you can't feel it but you just gotta believe me, ok? I'm not crazy — or maybe I am but it's not my fault. So, hey, can I come crash in my old bedroom till I die?"

A care facility would be nice, I thought — have my meals brought to me, my room cleaned, bedsheets washed — no need to worry about driving places or going shopping. But a care facility cost money, and I knew my parents would never agree to put me up in one. They hated to spend money…

Unless… maybe there is a way…

I realized I needed to do something serious, something dangerous, so my parents would be *forced* to put me somewhere to keep me safe. To keep others safe from me.

The wound on my arm healed quickly, and I felt a little bad for scaring my family, but not bad enough to change my plan. The medical staff in the hospital crisis wing were kind, quickly becoming unwitting supporters of my deception.

I complained of hallucinations and voices that told me to hurt myself and others. I described missing time, pounding headaches, and confusion. The usual stuff. I needed to be sure I was seen as a problem, that I needed to be secreted away where no one would have to deal with me. I needed to be sure they wouldn't just try and medicate it all away. I needed to be safe while I waited. I needed someone to take care of me for a long, long time.

It wasn't really a lie. The bricks *are* a particularly persistent — and solid — hallucination.

I've stopped counting the bricks now. There are too many; I lose count when I try. My bed is positioned so that the door to my room is in my sight hole when I lay down.

My voice sounds weird when I speak. It reverberates, bouncing off the bricks, as if I were speaking into the side of a house. The bricks eliminate most outside sound and beyond the boundaries of my room, I can't hear much. The orderlies talk to me through the ever-shrinking hole, always accommodating my 'delusions'; it's the only thing that sounds normal anymore.

I've made a friend, somehow. Danica and I watch *The Voice* every Tuesday. She doesn't think it's strange that I sit with my body twisted in the chair just right so I can see the TV screen. I told

Danica about the bricks when I'd been here for three months. She listened quietly from somewhere behind the wall where I couldn't see her, and when I was finished, she told me about the gnomes that stole cash from her mother's wallet when she was a kid, something she was always blamed for.

Why do I not believe her? It's not like my story is any less unbelievable, but for some reason hers feels… I don't know… *really* unbelievable.

I feel like a hypocrite.

The bricks are going to kill me.

This morning, I woke up to a new brick resting above me, in the air, touching the topmost brick at the corner.

A ceiling! They're starting a ceiling! They're walling me into a box! Waves of nausea pulse through my body. Deferring the horror is no longer an option. I know what's coming. I'm going to be bricked in here. Alive.

I don't feel the breeze from the ceiling fan on my skin anymore. My breathing is thin and labored. With the new brick ceiling closing slowly above me, my air is running out. I finally asked the nurses for an oxygen tank after weeks of suffering in silence. I'd almost forgotten they were here to help me.

The tank would probably get in my way if I had any sort of life anymore. Here, in the silent dark, it's almost like having a friend. Danica gave me a yellow smiley face sticker, and I put it on my mask. Now people outside can't see my face any better than I can see theirs.

I know the nurses think this is all in my head and I don't blame them. Danica doesn't see the bricks either. Jared and Kendra never did. Just me. The scars on my hands are real — Danica can see *them*. She asked about them. I don't understand how she can see my scars but not my bricks.

I wish just *one* other person would say they could see them too. The nurses play along, of course, as it is their job to do. They bring me fresh oxygen tanks, leave the lights on after that horrible night I woke up to pee and couldn't find the light switch in the dark. But their tolerance of my strange needs does nothing to affirm my torturous reality.

Really, the oxygen and lights and assistance are nice, but I just want to hear someone say they believe me; truly believe, not the way you *say* you believe someone just to talk them down, when really you think they're full of shit. The bricks have isolated me from any sort of real comfort. How can I ever be fully seen and understood when my reality is invisible to everyone around me?

I have an awful lot of time to ruminate, these days, between an endless supply of paperbacks and

3D puzzles. The nurses even gave me a little headlamp when I complained of the dark. I'm sure they laugh together about it while they eat their lunch in the breakroom. The truth is, I would give up all these little luxuries — the books, the puzzles, even the Nintendo Switch — just for one of them to look at me and truly understand.

There's one space left. Just enough room for one last brick. I lie curled up in my box and stare at it for hours each day, the light streaming in through my last portal to the outside world. Yes, people can bring me supplies. I will not starve. They can bring my food tray to me, put it in my hands, remove it when I'm done, lead me to the bathroom. They can give me fresh oxygen tanks, hook them up for me.

But I'm not truly breathing. I've known this for a long time.

Even with the oxygen, I feel like I'm suffocating. I wonder, when the last brick falls into place, will it cut off the sounds of the room around me? Will I be able to hear people speaking to me, asking what I need, if they're outside my personal prison?

What if when that last brick falls into place, no one will be able to *hear me?* What if no one can hear me ask for a fresh tank? For food?

What if no one can hear me cry out?

For Evan

CINDERELLA AUCTION

In the fall of 2023, I read Stephen King's On Writing. He was quite insistent that I at least try writing if I thought it would be something I enjoyed. I had written in the past when I was younger, but never seriously or with publication in mind. This story was my first step, created during a ten-minute free write session. It's very odd, and it's (again) based pretty much entirely off a nightmare, this one about cars being auctioned off while covered in gore from accidents. It's rough, sophomoric, and a little childish, but it means a lot to me. It started me on the path I walk today.

Lots of people in movies get real upset when their parents decide their working future for them, trying to pass on the family business and all. Everyone always wants to be something big, as if your life isn't worth something unless you go to college.

What the fuck are these people thinking?

I wouldn't say I had a passion for cars or that I was a natural at fixing them up. But if someone is willing to give you a job the minute you start asking for toys that cost more than fifteen dollars a piece (almost all of them these days, except that crappy mass-produced shit made by little kids in China, God save us), you're set up for life.

Work isn't supposed to be about passion. It isn't natural. The only people who believe that are the ones working you like a horse in the heat. Work is about getting by.

Dad had been telling me since I was old enough to understand—and probably way before that, though I can't tell you for certain—that when I grew up and had the strong hands for it I'd be getting his mechanic shop from him. As a five-year-old, I was just happy to be bouncing on my dad's knee. As a fourteen-year-old, I realized this meant I absolutely *had it made.*

No fussing around with things like college, resumes, 401k's and all that nonsense. I'd inherit a business already established, funded, and with a clientele to keep me above water three lifetimes over- just about every one of those college graduates in town who write resumes and use whatever a 401k is. They don't teach you how to deal with a piston failure or how to re-gap a spark plug in college. Well, I guess if they did, I wouldn't know it anyway.

By the time I was fourteen and getting interested in girls and how to get them, me and Dad already had a bright red '02 Camaro all souped-up and ready for a little lady to warm the passenger seat (usually it turned out to be my no-good school buds who couldn't be bothered to fix up their own damn cars). I also had damn near three thousand dollars in my Iowa National savings account, saved up from being Dad's only employee—all off the books, of course.

The last decade or so since then I'd been learning everything there is to know from Dad, not just about fixing up those college dips' toys, but also about running a business.

We'd go out on "field trips" once I was in high school or so. He'd take me to see Dan, his accountant, or as Dad called him in private, Fat Dan (man was no less than four hundred pounds), and Fat Dan would explain how to make sure my books were balanced and keep the IRS off my back. Great guy.

Sometimes we'd go hundreds of miles in the pickup to buy a specific hunk of metal from some hick a state away. The road trips were a hoot with Dad, and as soon as we got that thing towed back into the shop we'd start making her good again. That was the satisfaction for me—turning something broken back into a running machine.

On a burning hot day in mid-July dad took me on a field trip. He called it a "Cinderella auction". Said it's a great way to get spare parts just about as cheap as those kid-made Chinese gadgets.

I was always up for learning something new from Dad, and field trips were almost always a great time, but I did secretly groan a little on the inside when he came into my room that morning. My sleep the night before had been terrible. Awful dream I'd had.

My current lady, Kelly, and I had been in my red Camaro. I thought I was really there at first, since there were lots of details I didn't think my dream-brain could come up with. I could feel the rivets on the steering wheel cover I'd bought the week before. Kelly's lips and tongue were stained blue from a slushie I somehow knew she'd drank at the movies. Crazy how much detail dreams can have.

We were in the Camaro, I assume heading back to her place, and she was laughing about something. She grabbed my hand and squeezed it. I opened my mouth to tell her I loved her when I saw a deer show up out of nowhere right there in front of us on the road. It turned to me and I saw my headlights reflect in its eyes. I yanked the wheel to the right, but it ran the wrong way and I hit it full-on. It came to a shattering stop against the windshield, which thankfully held against it. I woke up right before we slammed head-first into a telephone pole I hadn't seen coming, being so focused on the deer and trying not to hit it.

It felt so real. What made me stay awake the rest of the night was this overwhelming BAD feeling, like the sky should've been red with ill omens or some shit like that.

I couldn't go back to sleep after. At some point I managed to slip into something like a half-doze, but Dad came in and let me know we were doing a field trip right when I felt like I could finally tip off.

I must've been more tired than I thought, 'cause I dozed the whole car ride there. When we stopped, I couldn't recall how far we had gone, or what part of town we were in.

We had pulled into a plain gravel parking lot with white chalked-in parking lines. The lot was almost full, maybe 25 cars in all. A few clusters of people were walking toward a big open blue building with "Eltopia Auction House" painted in red letters across the front. Below that and to its right was a hastily attached canvas banner that screamed

AUCTION TODAY!!

I had never been to an auction before. I knew Dad used to go sometimes, but I think it was more for the fun of it than anything, since he never brought home any purchases. Dad and I got in line to get a paddle.

"What are we biddin' on, Dad? Is this a car auction?" I asked.

Dad stayed quiet for long enough to make me think he didn't hear me, but when I started to ask again he turned to me.

"It is, but it's a special kind. Did you have any breakfast before we left?"

"Huh-uh. How come, Dad? Are we gonna be here for a while?" I asked.

"Probably."

Something about his tone was making me nervous. It was how he sounded the day Ranger got hit. I was in middle school, and I came home to him sitting at the table. He talked in a careful, kind of gentle way, like he was afraid he'd break me or blow me away or something. He asked about school, if I learned anything. He and I were both of the same opinion that school was a waste of time for me (aside from the basics I had already learned) and he hadn't asked about school in years.

Of course, eventually I realized he was just fixing to tell me about Ranger but was beating around it 'cause he didn't want me to be upset.

It unsettled me how much he sounded like he did that day right then. That odd feeling from my dream was starting to make its way into my head, that slight feeling of BAD. Not to mention I was rapidly feeling more tired with each minute we stood there waiting in line. They combined to form a hot anxious pit in my stomach.

Assuming he was waiting until the "right time" to say whatever he was saving up for me, I decided not to ask Dad any more questions for a while. Best he just worked on getting it out.

After they gave dad his paddle, I followed him and the rest of the bidders through the building and outside. My eyes had adjusted to the milder light inside, so when we stepped out into that big empty gravel lot the sun stabbed through my tired eyes and I had to hold my hand over them for a bit before they stopped hurting.

I was so exhausted I was starting to feel nauseous.

Why did it feel like I hadn't slept a second the night before?

Instead of a stage and chairs for the auctioneer and bidders like I had been expecting, the bidders were standing in a loose, somewhat uneasy-looking crowd facing the gravel lot.

As Dad and I stepped up to join them in the back, I asked, "Where are all the cars, Dad? Are we super early?"

"They'll be along soon."

He seemed to think hard about something for a moment.

"Do you remember last Christmas, when we visited Grandma?" he asked.

I wrinkled my brow at him. "Uh, yeah? 'Course I do. Aunt Lori fell going down to get extra blankets from the basement laundry. Can't forget a thing like that so quick. Why, Dad?" That anxious hole in my stomach suddenly filled itself with white-hot fear. "Why? Did Grandma fall? Is something wrong?"

Dad chuckled at my sudden alarm and shook his head. "Grandma's okay, bud. You remember all that blood when Lori fell?"

I nodded. "Yeah. Funny how much you bleed when it's your face. I thought for sure she was done for." The image of the blood on the staircase made my stomach feel even worse.

Dad's voice dropped a little, and he started using that overly-gentle tone again. "How'd you do with the blood? I didn't take much note of anything besides getting Lori up the stairs." He glanced around casually. "It give you nightmares?"

His demeanor was really starting to put me off. The mention of nightmares while mine from a few hours ago still hadn't quite faded away made me wonder if I had yelled out in the night. I wished he'd just get to the point, 'cause I was starting to sweat from the anxiety, and my heart was fluttering like a bird.

I was about to ask him what the hell he was trying to get at when a smell wafted over us on a light breeze that seemed to come out of nowhere. At the same time, I heard the gravel crunching under tires not too far off.

The smell started out faint. At first it was a kind of murky smell, like your privates start to get after three or so days missing a shower. I thought it was the sweaty hillbilly-looking dude a few feet in front of us.

Then it came closer, and it got stronger.

It reminded me a little of before we got Ranger spayed. I was just a little too young to understand exactly what was going on, but what got through to me at the time was that Ranger wanted to have pups but she hadn't gotten any, and that hurt her tummy somehow, 'cause I kept finding little blood spots on places she'd been laying.

They didn't smell like the blood from those nose bleeds I used to get when I was five. It was like fermented blood, like it had been deep inside her cooking from the heat of her body. It was a very internal smell.

That same kind of deep, rich smell seemed to be coming with whatever was driving our way on the gravel. It sounded heavy, and I thought I could hear multiple vehicles.

There was something really, really wrong with that smell.

A hot finger of dread started in my chest and spread up to my throat. That feeling of BAD, of wrongness, from my nightmare started to fill the air like the spray from a skunk. All at once I needed to get out of there. I did not want to see what was on its way over to us.

I grabbed Dad, almost clutching him like a drowning man. "I don't feel good. I think I'm gonna pass out or something. Can we forget it and head home?"

Dad seemed to ignore me. He was staring raptly to the left, the direction where the sound and smell was coming from. It was like he needed to see what was approaching as desperately as I needed to get out of there.

I wanted to just turn around and go back to the car and wait for him. I was starting to think maybe that dread, rotten feeling I had meant I was having one of those warning premonitions, like the people who worked at the towers and called out sick on 9/11. While there was a curious part of me that wanted to know why Dad had brought me here and seemed so serious, I wanted to get us both out of there as soon as possible.

"Please, Dad," I said. "What's going on?"

His voice sounded numb and far away. "It's called a Cinderella auction."

"Dad, what are we bidding on?"

As if in response, a heavy duty rusty white truck pulled into view from the left. The smell became so strong I had to cover my nose to prevent myself from gagging. It was so thick, I felt like I was choking on it.

It was too rich. Like when you eat a whole slice of chocolate cake with no milk to cut through it. And it was absolutely putrid.

It was too private, too intimate. Not something people are meant to smell. My instincts rebelled against it.

This shouldn't be, I thought.

The truck was hauling a long flatbed. Strapped to the flatbed were cars. What was left of them.

It took up our whole field of view and came to a stop in a position where all the bidders could get a good look. I couldn't see the driver at all.

And I saw what was causing the smell.

Every car on the flatbed was covered in blood.

Revulsion rose up in me, and I tried to scream, but when I opened my mouth only a kind of silent wheeze came out. Like when you try to scream in a nightmare.

"It's called a Cinderella auction," Dad repeated. "They're cars that were wrecked in fatal crashes. People buy 'em for the parts."

Seemingly from miles away, the rapid river of words signature to an experienced auctioneer started up. I look around but couldn't tell which person on the gravel was doing it. My dad went on quietly.

"They sell 'em for dirt cheap 'cause of all the mess. Be a waste to scrap 'em without taking out any good parts first."

I gaped at him. This was wrong, almost sacrilegious, auctioning off cars that people had died in. Had bled in. It was BAD.

The sky had at some point taken on a slightly orange tint. The midday sun was much too bright for a darkening sky. It was burning

cooking all that blood

my skin, making me sweat even more.

"I don't like it. I don't want to touch parts from something… like that," I said.

Dad finally tore his eyes from the flatbed and looked at me. He looked mildly amused. "What? It's not like they're haunted. We'll clean everything off first, if you want," he offered.

I forced myself to look back at the flatbed. There was a white pickup whose entire front end was smashed in. The windshield was folded in on itself. It had two large, distinct holes in the glass, both bloody around the edges.

There was a blue mid-2000's sedan behind it, except it was missing everything that should've gone in front of the front seats, which were stained a sickly brown all over, the color of old blood not yet scrubbed out. Something textured the top edge of the seat on the driver's side. It was lumpy and an indistinguishable color, gray or brownish maybe.

It took me several seconds to understand that it was brain matter. That car still had its driver's brains on it, and we were all there to bid on it.

And boy, people were bidding. I came out of my horror to the sound of the auctioneer going off like a gatling gun, and people throughout the crowd were raising and lowering their paddles eagerly.

It was too much for me, and I swooned a bit. Dad grabbed me firmly by one arm and supported me as I fought to stay conscious. He did it almost automatically, like my reaction to this was as every day as the newspaper funnies.

Time blurred for me, and images were flicking in front of my eyes like someone clicking through their camera roll. In each shutter, the sky seemed to be turning more red.

I drifted fully away for a short time, and my mind replayed the last few seconds of my dream from the night before. The deer turned, smashed into the Camaro again, and I saw the telephone pole running toward us. I heard Kelly scream again.

It seemed like that was what jolted me awake. For a moment I thought it was real, that someone in the crowd had finally come to their senses and had enough, screaming because this was wrong, it was BAD. But everyone's attention was still on the flatbed and paddles were still bobbing up and down like a fucked up game of whack-a-mole.

They must have sold everything on that flatbed, because it started to pull away. It circled around and drove behind us, where it parked. I didn't think the smell could get any worse.

Another flatbed pulled up from the left.

The cars on this on were just as bloody as the first ones. They were wrecked so severely that I couldn't even begin to guess how they had been hit. How their occupants had died.

The auctioneer started up again as if he had never stopped. He spat words rapidly and the words increased in intensity, like the religious throes of a cultist.

I decided to try Dad one more time. "This is wrong. Can't you feel it?" He didn't budge. I smacked him lightly on the shoulder. "Dad, I think there's something wrong with the sky. Look."

Dad glanced at me and looked away. His voice was starting to sound almost fuzzy. "We need spare parts. Money's tight. Sorry bud." As if to emphasize his point, he raised his paddle at the auctioneer. "It's just business."

"Dad. The sky." It was the shade of

blood

a ripe tomato. I saw his eyes briefly flick up, then back at the flatbed again. He was silent.

I was starting to get frustrated. Surely he had noticed the reddening sky. It was casting everything in a kind of rosy light, like I was peering at everything through a cut ruby. "Dad! What is that? Is it a storm, or a tornado or something?" I felt six years old again. The second flatbed started pulling away.

Out of nowhere it felt like my forehead had been set on fire. A wave of pure terror passed through me, and I thought I would vomit from it. Under the sound of the crunching gravel rose a kind of humming sound, like the tension I was feeling coming toward us was starting to physically manifest itself. The sound could have even been coming from me, I couldn't tell.

From what seemed like another plane of existence, I heard my dad mutter, "Here we go. That's the one."

I tore my attention away from that apocalyptic sky back down. A new flatbed was pulling in.

There was a bright red pile of metal and glass in its middle, all by itself. Kelly's scream echoed through my head again. At once the temperature climbed by at least ten degrees. I felt like I was going to start blistering, like we were all being cooked under the sky, that red sky. Red like the burners inside an oven, and we were inside with the dials cranked up.

The crowd gasped collectively, and turned around, looking directly at me. Some wore faces of disgust, others sadness, some a type of calm acceptance.

I stared back at them, unsure what to do or how to react. This defied reason and logic.

Am I dreaming? I wondered.

I reached out for Dad again. Grasping his shoulder, feeling the cloth of his old white T-shirt under my fingers.

This feels real. But it can't be.

Dad looked at me. A silent tear was tracing a path down his cheek.

All at once, he and the crowd raised a hand and pointed at the flatbed, never taking their gazes from my face. Their other hands raised their paddles. All of them.

I could hear the sneering voice of the auctioneer, but it sounded too slow and deep, like a record player switched to the wrong RPM setting.

The insane behavior of the bidders had taken my attention off the flatbed momentarily. I studied the red chunk of metal closer.

It was bright red. There was a massive gash in the hood, and blood went up the windshield in large splotches. Something was stuck in the ruined mess of the grill. Hair? Short, mousy brown. A deer?

I looked back at the hauntingly still bidders, holding me captive with their gazes.

Wait…

I blinked and looked at the car again. An icy hot finger of terror and realization slid up my spine. The rims.

My rims.

Remains of sheep skin seat covers, now covered in blood. Not just stains. It was pooling in the seats, like it was being drained out of an invisible faucet. The humming noise crescendoed. It became as loud as the stench of the blood. Over the sound, I could hear Dad begin to weep bitterly.

It was my Camaro. Shattered. Broken. Smash-ed.

Bloody.

Just as it became unbearable and I felt something inside my head *pop*, everything went red.

I'm back in my dream. The rivets on the steering wheel cover under my touch.

The deer
SMASH
I'm swerving-
The telephone pole

Pain
blackness
smell of blood. fermented. intimate. too rich

For Stephen King, who will never read this

THE GUARDIAN

This was part of my Halloween posts in 2025 on Pen & Sword. I really enjoyed getting nasty with gore here, and I think it's a fun and quick romp with maybe a little something to say about man and nature. It's also gross!

The Guardian was there when the land was formed.

She was there when the Earth turned cold and the people came across the great land bridge to the north. She saw them move across the continent, searching for warmth, for plants and game. She opened her arms to these cold, curious people and found that she loved them. More than the trees and the lakes and the fish and deer and hedgehogs.

For they could love in the way that she could love.

The people loved her land, loved her trees and lakes and fish and deer and hedgehogs. They cared for the land, only taking what they had to to survive, leaving enough for the land and lakes to recover each time.

The Guardian kissed each of these people on the brow when they came into the world and in return they gave her worship and respected her land.

It was this way for centuries, and the Guardian was happy and her people were happy.

Then came the others.

The Guardian was there when the others came. Not by the land bridge; it had long since vanished. They came across the ocean, ferried by other forces with whom she did not associate.

She was there when the others found her land and decided to stay, decided to bring more of their people to her land.

The Guardian found that these others could love, but not in the way that her people loved.

The others loved power, loved domination, loved stepping on one another to rise. After centuries among her people, she had learned to see into the hearts of men.

What she saw in the hearts of the others was not love for her trees and lakes and fish and deer and hedgehogs. The others loved her land for what it could do for their power, their domination, their race to rise above others.

The Guardian saw the others, saw into their hearts, and understood that they would only bring suffering, imbalance, and pain. Pain to her people, who would fall to their strange diseases like rotting tree roots.

The Guardian decided, after long months of thought and meditation, that she must drive the others away. She would not use her people to do so; she understood the stain it might leave on their souls.

She would use her creatures, the unspeaking ones who dwelled in her forest.

Richard hauled his kill toward the wooden palisade that marked the edges of the settlement.

The deer, which had been alive and pumping blood less than two hours before, now hung limp and cooling from Richard's shoulders.

"Richard!" cried his wife, spotting his app-roach. "Your hunt was bountiful?"

He nodded, slinging the carcass down onto the cold, dying grass. Soon the ground would be too hard to dig in. He hoped they didn't lose anyone to the frost in the winter: none of them had much knowledge of the climate here. It was a new world, after all.

Richard stepped toward his wife and kissed her quickly on the cheek in greeting. When he pulled away and looked at her face, he saw a strange expression take it over.

"Richard?" she said, voice thin and trembling. "What…"

His wife cut off, eyes wide and staring behind him.

Richard turned around, hand going for the hunting rifle slung across his back. But when he saw what his wife had seen, his entire body froze.

The deer, which Richard had shot dead less than two hours before, now stood on its feet, bloodied but fully alive, the fatal gunshot still shining like a star from its forehead.

Richard could not speak, only made a choked sound of surprise and disbelief.

Then the deer darted forward, straight for Richard.

Richard screamed as the deer smashed its thick skull into his hips, the impact so strong with unnatural force that his internal organs burst like overfilled sacks and his pelvic bone cracked in three places.

Richard crumpled to the cold ground, the dying grass scratching his face as he screamed until his throat bled, writhing and pissing and wishing for his mother.

His wife was paralyzed, not believing or even understanding what she had just seen.

When the deer charged again, she only stood, unmoving, too deep in the shock and madness in which her mind sheltered her. One ram from the deer's head destroyed her womb, her uterus, her liver and kidneys.

Richard and his wife laid on the hard ground and died slowly and very painfully beside each other, too deep in their own agonies to realize the other was right there beside them.

While Richard and his wife died, an eagle dropped down from the sky over the settlement. It angled toward Henry, who was gutting a rabbit by torchlight with a dull knife. They were supposed to get fresh supplies soon, so Henry had to make do with the nearly-useless tool.

Henry screamed as the eagle descended, digging its deadly-sharp talons into the slippery skin that covered Henry's skull, then took to the skies with great force and swiftness, taking most of the skin from Henry's head with it. It dripped blood down to the earth as the eagle flew away, screeching with the rapture of a good hunt.

Henry died from the shock, as his heart was already defective and sensitive to stress.

Margaret saw the skin yanked from Henry's head like a fur cap from her seat by the cookfire. She sprang to her feet and turned to run, though where she planned to run she did not know, but as she reached the trees lining one side of the settlement, she literally ran headfirst into a bear, who was already up on hind legs.

The bear roared, and when it snapped its deadly jaws shut, it did so over the face of Margaret, who struggled for a few moments, then stilled, hanging limply from the bear's jaws.

The rest of the settlement was destroyed in a similar manner as the creatures of the forest and plains converged on them, guided by orders from the Guardian.

The Guardian spared only the eleven children of the settlement, using wolves to chase them away from the massacre and guide them toward her own people, who would take them in and raise them to love the land and not use it for their own selfish gain.

When the massacre was finished, the Guardian ordered her creatures to take the bodies with them, back to their burrows and nests and caves, where they could make use of their bones and tissue. Her land was safe once again, and the Guardian came down to the Earth. She walked the settlement, inspecting the way these others had tried to live. A barrier of trees cut from her forests guarded its borders on three sides. She raised one hand and sharpened it to a point, then leaned down and carved a word into one of the posts.

It was a single word, one that meant 'guardian of balance' in a tongue that none but her people would understand. When she finished, she smiled and ascended back to her place in the trees, where she would guard her people as long as it was in her power to do so.

The word was CROATOAN.

For my mom

SCOUT'S HONOR

I've got no fun origin story for this one, but I would like to thank my dad for his essential contribution to it- he helped me out with the title, and suggested adding the Boy Scouts element. I think it was really the icing on the cake that is this story. It's one of my darker ones. Might want to keep a light on.

When Gio and Marcus plunge into the cold blackness of the South Pacific at two in the mor-ning, the impact of the water nearly tearing the skin from their exposed faces, they expect to die shortly after.

They do not.

As if by a miracle, the two men explode into the water like falling stars not ten feet from one another. The angry ocean water shocks them, spins them around, altering their perception of up and down.

Marcus opens his mouth to scream, not only at the shock of the cold, but at the shock of everything- the Japanese plane flying straight for their own, the heat of the fire, the tearing of his eardrums as his entire world exploded and plunged him into a watery hell.

Marcus is the first to find the surface after finally forcing his eyes to open in the cold salt-water. He specifically hates opening his eyes under-water, something all of his friends back home in Michigan could do in the pool. Something that made him feel vulnerable, naked, as the soft balls in his skull were coated in the chemical and bacteria-ridden water.

He opens his eyes here, now, in the South Pacific at two in the morning, because he knows he must.

Marcus kicks his feet, wooden and numb from shock or cold or both, and propels himself toward the pulsing orange lights he sees through the distorting waves. The saltwater stings his eyes, makes them feel like ice cubes stuck in his brain, but he pushes on, breaching the surface like a whale. He sucks in air with a raw throat, drinking it in with harsh gasps.

He treads water, spinning around, taking in his situation. The orange lights he saw from below the surface turn out to be flaming bits of plane, his or the Japanese, or perhaps both. Not that it matters anymore.

His ears are still ringing from the explosion, but his eyes clear of saltwater quickly. And he sees a churning in the water ten feet away, nearer to the flaming wreckage, the fires slowly dying as the saltwater laps over them.

"Gio!"

Marcus swims toward the spot. When he is nearly upon it, the surface breaks in a shattering white burst and there is Gio, wet and red-faced and utterly confused, but alive.

"Gio!" Marcus shouts, reaching out and grasping the arm of his gunner with one hand while using the other to keep himself afloat.

Gio coughs and almost goes under again several times before his eyes clear. They land on Marcus and go wide.

"Marcus?"

"Are you hurt?" Marcus shouts over the roar of the ocean and the distant battle, now quite far away, as their flight from the pursuing Japanese plane separated them from the main throng by a considerable distance.

Gio does not respond, only looks around him wildly, flailing his arms in the water.

He must not be a good swimmer, Marcus thinks.

"Over here!" Marcus calls over the din, then begins to swim for the nearest piece of debris.

The chunk of plane is charred black from the now-quenched flames. It is metal and something softer, and it floats like a rubber duck in a bathtub, bobbing along without much care.

Marcus is upon it by the time he understands it is the bottom cushion of one of their seats, still welded into a scrap of steel underbelly. The entire piece looks to be about eight feet long, give or take.

It will float. Their seat cushions were designed to do so, for situations exactly like this.

Marcus thrusts a hand up onto the seat. He struggles for several tense moments to pull himself up onto the improvised floatation device, as there is nothing he can push against with his feet, only the deep, unfathomable depths of blackness that fill the Pacific Ocean.

Finally, he clambers up onto the piece and screams in pain. The edges of the broken steel are raw and sharp as any razor, and he's drawn his right thigh right over one of its jagged teeth.

Marcus curls in on himself on the floating steel, grunting in pain as hot blood pumps from the wound, nearly the entire length of his thigh. It warms him as it pools under his back, an absurd relief among the agony.

Then Marcus hears a shout and a wet slap, and it pulls him back to himself.

It's Gio. He's struggling to pull himself up onto the scrap beside Marcus. Despite his injury, Marcus forces himself to sit up and lean over, grabbing onto Gio's arms with every ounce of strength left in him. It isn't easy, and they nearly tip the whole thing over before Gio flips himself up and onto his back, coughing.

The two men sprawl across the scrap of floating metal for several minutes before they are recovered enough to speak with one another.

"Crazy son of a bitch," Gio pants, "Flew right into us. Killed himself. Fucking crazy."

Marcus nods, cringing from the pain in his leg. The saltwater lapping up into the wound stings with every wave. "I've heard of it. They're called kamikaze."

"Comic-ozzie?" Gio mutters, his teeth beginning to rattle as the cold night air sets deep in his bones.

Marcus ignores him. "We have to get help. I'm… I'm bleeding."

Gio glances down and sees the wound in his pilot's leg for the first time. "Goddamn, Marcus! That happen in the… the crash?"

Marcus shakes his head. "Cut it open climbing onto this thing. Surprised you didn't cut yourself on it, too."

Gio looks down at himself and freezes. Marcus looks at his gunner more closely in the near-darkness.

The bottom of Gio's white shirt, standard issue for fliers, is dark with scarlet blood.

"Oh, shit," Gio mutters, then makes a sound like choking. Marcus tenses before he realizes he is laughing.

"Gio, we've got to do something," Marcus urges, trying to get his comrade to focus. "We're both going to bleed out if we just sit here. And we're far away enough from the island…" He looks off in the distance, unsure where the island lay now. "I don't know how long it'll take them to find us."

"I don't know if I can swim anywhere," Gio says. His breath is coming more quickly now that he's aware of his wound, his panic building.

Marcus fights down his own panic as he considers how dire their situation really is. Nothing in sight but the wreckage of planes, one American, one Japanese. Likely a corpse sinks down into the endless abyss below them. Likely it's in several pieces.

He thinks in this moment of his baby brother, Henry. Sweet Henry who wouldn't go along hunting with Marcus and their father because he couldn't bring himself to harm a deer. Henry, who still held Marcus's hand in moments of anxiety, who saved up all his money selling magazines after school just to buy two tickets to see the local symphony perform Tchaikovsky's Nutcracker after Marcus mentioned wanting to go. Henry, who begged Marcus to join their local chapter of the Boy Scouts of America with him so he would have at least one friend there.

Sweet Henry, who was seventeen, barely too young to pledge himself to service. Henry, who had cried at the bus station and made Marcus promise to come back.

"I promise, Henry."

"Scout's honor?" Henry had sniffed through his tears. Henry had never been ashamed to cry; their father hadn't been there to instill that lesson.

Marcus had smiled and lifted his right hand in the old Boy Scout salute, his palm facing Henry and thumb holding his pinkie down.

"Scout's honor," Marcus had promised.

Marcus realizes with cold numbness that he will be breaking that promise after all.

It is two in the morning in the middle of the South Pacific, and Marcus and Gio have been shot down nearly thirty miles from their last known location.

Marcus begins to cry.

The two fallen airmen drift on the crashing waves for three hours before they see the ship.

Marcus doesn't believe the ship is real at first. He's lost blood and his vision blurs in and out of focus. Gio hasn't spoken for some time. Their throats are raw and coppery from shouting for help.

"Gio?" he ventures with a voice like sharp glass.

Gio sits up suddenly. He has seen it, too. "Is that… a ship?"

The ship floats stoically on the water quite close to them. Neither saw it approach, which makes no sense to Marcus. It's nothing but flat waves here. Nothing that large could sneak up on them.

We both must have been drifting off while it approached, Marcus reasons. It both comforts and alarms him. Drifting off is not good; they have both lost a considerable amount of blood.

"Hey!" Marcus shouts at the ship, sitting up and waving his arms wildly. "Hey! Help! Help us!"

Then Gio is up and shouting too, and neither of them feels like a fool with their arms waving about, shouting their throats to stinging pieces. This ship is salvation. Even if it isn't an American ship, something will happen to them. Either execution here in the water or being taken as prisoners of war is a more attractive prospect than slowly dying of exposure in the middle of the ocean.

Marcus screams until his voice is a buzzing rattle deep in his chest, the way his Grampy sounded in his last years before his diseased, leathery lungs gave out. Marcus makes this connection and finds it fitting- it is the voice of a doomed man.

Their efforts are rewarded, though it is hard to tell with the dark and distance.

The ship slinks toward them in the endless black water.

As it nears, Marcus is able to see it in greater detail. It is three-masted, large enough for a substantial crew. A flag waves from its main mast, though Marcus cannot make out in the early morning light which country she represents. From the general shape, build, and design of it, though, Marcus is quite sure it is European. And something is strange about it, aside from drifting silently in the South Pacific at five in the morning near the site of an air battle.

It is familiar to Marcus.

Like it has come to life from somewhere deep in his memories. Frustratingly, he cannot recall where.

All the same, the ship approaches the two marooned, bleeding airmen.

Then Gio speaks from beside him. "Looks like it sailed right out of my sophomore year history book."

That's it. Marcus understands what is so familiar about the ship. It's nearly identical to the ship on the cover of *Treasure Island*, a paperback lovingly battered from years of trading back and forth between him and Henry.

It's like it sailed right out of the past, Marcus thinks. It is a frightening thought, for reasons he doesn't understand.

The ship is upon them and Marcus can make out her name, painted lovingly in black script along her hull. Their savior is *Venus*.

Marcus and Gio cannot make out any sailors to greet them on the deck, though it is difficult to see from their position down below. They are just beginning to wonder aloud to each other just how they're expected to get on the ship when a shape falls from the deck and thumps to the water twenty feet from them.

Not eager to plunge their wounds back into the stinging saltwater, Marcus suggests they use their hands to paddle for the object rather than abandoning their makeshift lifeboat. As they approach the object, Marcus sees that it is a round item covered with aging canvas, tied to a rope connected to somewhere on the deck. Cork, possibly.

Not the classic red-and-white striped life ring Marcus would have expected. This object seems more rudimentary. Older.

Gio is able to grab the life ring first, smacking numb, pale fingers against the buoyant cork. He grabs it with both hands and grunts in pain.

"Gio?"

The gunner grimaces and shakes his head. "Hurts my stomach. Let's hope they pull us up quick."

Marcus sees no other life ring drop down and understands they're expecting to cling together to be lifted. With a nod, Gio gingerly pushes off from their makeshift raft and drops into the water, wherein he cries out again.

"That stings, oh good Jesus it stings," Gio pants.

Marcus feels sick for his friend, and hesitates before moving, afraid of a similar pain in his leg. Then he remembers it's likely this or die on this broken piece of plane.

He pushes off the debris and wraps his arms around Gio's shoulders, and they both groan with the pain.

Then the life ring quivers, and they are being lifted. Up and up, finally out of the water, much to their mutual relief. Their clothes are heavy on their frames as they drip, the sound loud as a waterfall in the silent morning. The two men, clumped together like ants on a candy, sway slightly as they are lifted, and Marcus fears they will be dashed against the side of *Venus*. They do not, but they come quite close.

Then hands grab their shoulders, first one set on Gio's, then another comes to help and pull Marcus as well. The world spins for the second time that day as the wounded men flip up and over the railing, twisting and coming to land on their backs. Marcus lies there for several seconds, eyes closed, praying thanks to God that now maybe, just maybe, he might keep his promise to Henry after all.

"What the—" Gio starts, and Marcus opens his eyes.

Sitting up, Marcus sees the railing he's just been pulled over. He sees fresh blood oozing lazily from his thigh. Turning his head, he sees the deck of a ship, much as he'd always imagined it.

There are sails, ropes, canvas everywhere. Wooden crates stacked haphazardly, a tall beam in the center with little steps built in for climbing. A cabin set into the stern end with the word "CAPTAIN" painted in that same black script. A structure with a door in the center of the deck, protecting a staircase that presumably leads belowdecks.

And not a single sailor.

"Hello?"

Marcus tries to keep the tremor out of his voice.

"Hello! Who has saved us? Please, we need a surgeon! We're wounded!" Marcus calls.

He looks to Gio and sees the man is horribly pale in the growing light of early morning. Gio's hands clutch the seeping wound in his stomach as he grunts in discomfort. Marcus realizes for the first time that he can smell Gio's wound: the metallic, rusty blood, the acid oozing from his lacerated organs, the partially-processed food and shit now leaking from his innards into his abdomen. Marcus holds back a retch. Retching will not make Gio feel any better.

"Help! Please! My friend is badly hurt!"

Still no response. His cries are absorbed by the damp wood of the deck and the canvas above them. Nobody stirs in the Captain's quarters, no feet thump up the wooden stairs from belowdecks.

"Good Jesus, oh good Jesus Christ," Gio is muttering between groans of pain. "Good Jesus, Marcus, who pulled us up? Who pulled us up?"

Marcus's blood freezes.

Who pulled us up?

He clearly remembers seeing the arms reaching for his shoulders. Clad in some filthy canvas material. Homespun, if he was remembering correctly. The bare hands—he thinks they were Caucasian.

"Somebody has to be here," Marcus mutters without much conviction. "Somebody who can help."

Gio shakes his head and continues to clutch at his stomach, muttering phrases under his breath, "Oh good Jesus, sweet Jesus, please, Jesus…"

Marcus is disturbed by quite a few things in this moment, but none are more horrifying than the utter terror he hears in Gio's voice, his unending, rhythmic mutterings reminiscent of a madman.

"I'm going to check the ship. I'll find someone. I'll be right back, Gio."

Marcus grunts as he pulls himself to his feet, shudders as more blood trickles down his sopping pants leg.

He looks about and sees a discarded canvas lying atop a crate. Pulling it free, Marcus brings it over to Gio and lays it over him gently, like a blanket.

"I'll find someone," he says again, then rises.

The door to the Captain's quarters is unlocked. Marcus pushes the door open and sticks his head inside. There is an oil lamp on a writing desk which is bolted to the floor. A bed hangs from ropes mounted to the ceiling. A pair of leather boots with no maker's mark sits ready and oiled by a carved wardrobe, which, upon inspection, is filled with fine clothes and a few warm-looking cloaks. Shivering, though more from blood loss than temperature, Marcus drapes one over his shoulders. He also takes a white shirt from its hanger and wraps it tightly around his wounded thigh like he learned in the Boy Scouts with Henry, tying the sleeves together as tight as he can and gritting his teeth. He is still amazed at his luck with the wound; though it hurts, it appears to have missed the femoral artery. He'd be dead by now if it were otherwise.

The Captain's quarters are empty. Clean, well-maintained, no signs of strife or struggle, but unquestionably empty.

Marcus leaves, a bitter taste in his mouth. He thinks it is fear.

Belowdecks Marcus finds a galley, which disturbs him on quite a new level. The tables are stacked with plates, many of which have slid off and broken, but many more that have stayed in place. The plates are covered in moldy, soupy, fetid-smelling remains of some meal, long congealed and turned vomit-brown on the porcelain. Marcus wrinkles his nose as soon as he enters the room.

Nobody is seated at the tables, laughing or spitting jokes or drinking, which Marcus has always pictured sailors doing. The ship tilts dramatically as a sizable wave shakes its entire being, and a bowl tips from the table nearest Marcus, splattering decayed, grub-infested slop that might've once been stew against his soaking standard-issue boots.

Now Marcus does retch, adding the last contents of his stomach to the general mess of the room. Marcus cannot handle being in here any longer, but he must know.

"Hello!" He calls out in the empty room. "I know you're here! Please! My friend needs help!"

Nothing.

Now beginning to weep tears of frustration, Marcus heads down the next staircase into the lower hold, which is completely dark, lacking any windows. He feels around blindly and finds what seem to be more wooden crates and some canvas sacks tied shut with rope. Supplies? Food? Marcus hopes it is usable, unlike the feast for dead men rotting upstairs.

He fumbles with the rope on one of the sacks, managing finally to untie it with shaking fingers. He cannot see, so he sticks his hand inside. Grain. Soft, lovely grain.

Then something moves against his splayed hand buried deep in the flour. Several somethings.

With a cry, Marcus yanks his hand from the maggot-infested flour and falls backward onto his rump. It hurts, but no more than slicing open his thigh did.

All gone bad, Marcus begins to think. *It's all gone bad. All the food. What will we eat?*

He stumbles up the stairs and emerges back into the newborn day. The ship is completely deserted, except for the maggots in the grain and flies that slowly devour the stinking food in the galley.

No one here. No one, Marcus thinks, shivering. *Who pulled us up?*

Gio is breathing quite alarmingly, shallow and quick. His face has turned red and hot, and the fluids leaking from his stomach wound smell fetid and foul. Like he has already begun to decompose.

"You're fine," Marcus repeats to his friend as he hauls him up as gently as he can, gripping him under his armpits. He does not like touching Gio-he is hot as a furnace. Too hot to mean anything good.

Marcus manages to haul Gio to the Captain's quarters, his friend mumbling in a fevered state the whole way: "Sweet Jesus. Please, oh please Jesus. Jesus Christ."

Gio barely reacts as Marcus lays him down beside the disappeared Captain's swinging bed, then struggles for nearly fifteen minutes to hoist the dying man up onto the cot. He is no longer worried about agitating the wound; a mucus-yellow film has collected and dried over the gash, a makeshift seal. Marcus thought at first that it was Gio's body healing the wound, then he caught the smell of it. Death. Rot. Decay.

"Oh, Gio," Marcus whispers, brushing the sweat-matted hair from his friend's pallid face. "Hang in there. Help will come soon."

Marcus does not mean this. The words don't seem to affect Gio anyway, as he groans weakly and calls for Jesus in hoarse whispers.

By the end of the day, Gio is dead.

The smell hanging over his ruined body now mingles with the odors of death, the shit and piss and blood turning to jelly in his veins.

Marcus does not accept this.

He checks in on Gio constantly, dabbing his paper-dry forehead with an embroidered handkerchief he found in the Captain's desk drawer. The initials "G.B." adorn the corner of the cloth, and Marcus spares only a moment to wonder about the Captain's name. He feels close, as if he is someone Marcus knows, having spent nearly twelve hours aboard his ship and wearing his coat.

"You know what'll fix you right up?" Marcus asks Gio, who does not stir. "Something to eat. Some grub, as sailors call it. You know, we're sailors now. Though this ship seems to really sail itself. But it's all the same." He has taken to talking for extended periods to Gio's glassy open eyes, rambling about the ship, his life, his brother Henry, his Grampy whose lungs went black and crumbled like coal.

"I'll see what I can whip up, Gio. Make you something to break that fever."

Marcus leaves Gio in G.B.'s bed for now, stopping on the deck for a long drink from the rainbarrel. It is brackish and gritty, despite having fallen fresh from the sky. He's already tried to give some to Gio, drenching one of the Captain's wool socks in the barrel and holding it to his friend's waxy lips. Gio did not drink, but Marcus gave him water patiently until he was satisfied.

Marcus makes his way belowdecks, lighting the old-style handlamp he found on G.B.'s desk with some strange looking sulfur sticks tucked into one drawer. In the hold, he can now see various scavengers and other varmints making themselves quite comfortable in the abandoned food supplies. Rats scurry across the floorboards, disappearing into holes gnawed in the wood of the crates. Flies buzz and flick to and fro over sacks of sugar, dried corn, and salted meat, laying eggs inside.

Marcus, nearly crazed with fear and denial, plunges a hand into the sugar sack after untying it, bringing up a cupped hand and eating the pure sugar straight. It crunches and pops under his teeth as he ingests the flies and maggots living inside, feeding.

Suddenly, he hears a roar from the sea outside, then the ship is tipping, and the crates scrape against the floorboards as the wrath of the South Pacific throws them around in the hold. Marcus goes flying as well, slamming into the wall with a bone-jarring thud. His hand lamp shatters, leaking tallow that catches briefly in the dying flame, then goes out.

Then a crate is tossed by one last jerk from the ocean and Marcus is screaming, blinding pain obliterating all other thought, as the crate smashes into him, impacting the hardest against his right shinbone, and Marcus thinks he hears his bone snap.

Marcus shrieks and tries to keep hold of himself, but fails. He drifts into blackness, unable to process the pain from the bone protruding from his lower leg.

For a time, Marcus knows only pain.

His mind wanders in and out of his past and his present, a fever dream borne from the burning of his mind. He sees himself feeding Henry as a baby, helping his mother who is laying down for an hour, she is just so tired. The spoon goes into Henry's perfect pink ribbon of a mouth, then Henry is eight years old and screaming in the grass after falling from the tire swing. It had been a hazard for years, their mother often said, and shouldn't have been played with in its state of decay. It's snapped, just like she always warned it would, and Henry smacks his head on the ground with the sound like a dropped watermelon. Marcus tries to comfort him, leaving his lead army men on the steps of the back porch when he hears the screams, but nobody calms Henry down as fast as their mother.

Marcus's mother. She hangs up laundry to dry on the line, whistling "Waltz of the Flowers" and spinning like a ballerina, thinking nobody is watching. She hugs him as he steps onto the bus, tears in her eyes as she tells him she is proud. Henry returns his Scout salute, shakes his hand, then thinks better of it and pulls Marcus in for a desperate hug. He calls out his name, shouting "Marcus! Marcus! Marcus!" And it is not a memory, it is right now.

Marcus snaps to full consciousness, and the pain is flowing back full force, but it does not matter, because someone is here, calling his name. It's coming from somewhere above.

"Hello," Marcus rasps, his voice thin and dry as the flowers his mother pressed into bookmarks. He clears his abused throat and tries again. "Hello?!"

"Marcus," the voice calls again, muffled by the layers of wood that make up the galley and deck of the ship above him.

"I'm down here! Please! My leg!"

There are thuds on the wood above. Marcus tries to sit up but falls back immediately, too weak to move. He has not eaten in over twenty-four hours. It must be nighttime, though he has no way of knowing in the full darkness of the hold. He misses the handlamp dearly. The darkness of the hold feels heavy. It pushes down on his chest and eyelids, and Marcus finds that he is crying, afraid of the dark like when he was a child.

The thuds make their way down the galley steps, and Marcus calls out in startled fear. Rationally, he knows that he is alone on *Venus*. "Who's there?"

The thuds stop just outside the doorway of the hold, where Marcus reasons the bottom of the stairs sit. There is silence. Marcus begins to shake. His leg sends spears of agony up his entire body. The pain has only increased with time.

"Please. Who's there? Gio? Is that you?"

Silence. Marcus cries, blubbering like a baby. Snot runs down his face, which has grown prickly with new hair growth in the time he's been here. "Please, it hurts so bad."

The voice is loud and hot, spoken directly into Marcus's ear. "Liar."

Marcus screams, throwing himself backward with his hands. His broken leg smacks into a crate, invisible in the utter darkness. The protruding bone makes direct impact with the wood and Marcus drifts away again.

Gio rots in the old Captain's bed as Marcus lays feverish, close to madness, in the utter darkness of the hold.

When he awakens again, he hears Henry talking on the deck above. "Come on, Ma, she's just a girl from my class. We're not getting married."

"I've seen how you look at her, Henry. It's puppy love at its finest," his mother responds with a teasing laugh.

Henry's voice becomes serious. "Marcus fancies her, Ma."

"You don't have to let him have everything," his mother says, a smile in her voice.

"I miss him."

Marcus starts.

"He broke his promise," his mother says. "He lied."

Henry's voice grows grave. "Yes. He lied to me. To you, to Gio. Poor Gio."

"He lied," his mother repeats.

"He gave Scout's Honor, he broke his promise," Henry hisses.

"No," Marcus whimpers, alone in the blackness. "No, I didn't. I tried. It wasn't my fault. It was the kamikaze!"

"LIES!" His brother and mother shout in unison from above.

"No, no, no," Marcus cries, shaking his head. He cannot see in the darkness that his mangled leg is turning purple.

Then the wet, wheezing sound of Grampy's breathing is beside him in the hold. Marcus screams, remembering the way Grampy looked in the last year of his life, thin and sallow and a burning cigarette clutched in fingers withered like talons.

The horrible, diseased breaths turn into chuckles, the sound like shucking corn in the fields behind their first house in Nebraska, where they lived until Marcus was five. The laughter rises and swells, then erupts into ear-splitting coughs that sound like lungs tearing themselves to pieces on glass. "You lied, boy," Grampy rattles from somewhere beside Marcus. "Death comes for us all. To promise otherwise is to bring it upon yourself."

Marcus screams until the dry skin of his throat rips, feeling those horrible, withered talons grab the skin of his shoulders and squeeze, tearing the flesh, sending streams of blood down Marcus's arms.

Gio rots in the old Captain's bed as Marcus dies screaming down below.

For my dad

SUNDAY

Madison wakes up on a Sunday morning at 7:30am, which is usual to her routine.

She visits the bathroom, wiping the sleep from her face with cotton pads drenched in witch hazel. Then it's into her closet, and she selects a burgundy activewear set, pulling the tight sports bra over her head and shimmying into the moisture-wicking leggings. She tops it with a breathable white active shirt, and she realizes if she doesn't leave right now she will walk into class late. Madison does her best to be on time to things, even if it doesn't always work out that way.

After slipping into her shoes and tossing a protein bar in her bag, Madison is out the door and in her car. She selects a playlist for the day, one designed to make Madison feel upbeat, invincible.

The drive to Pilates class is uneventful. There is the usual number of poor drivers, whom Madison curses to the empty car as they merge onto the highway too slowly, change lanes without signaling, drive ten miles per hour under the speed limit in the middle lane. To Madison, her world temporarily confined to only the recycled air of her Corolla, these injustices are grave, worthy of her bitterest vitriol. Green Day's *Horseshoes and Hand-grenades* blasts from the car's stock speakers as she scowls at a minivan that's weaving into her lane.

Probably on their phone, she thinks acidly.

Eventually, the drive concludes as Madison pulls into the parking lot of her Pilates studio, and then in ten minutes, she has entirely forgotten every injustice inflicted upon her during the drive, her irritation forgotten as she follows the instructor's directions, moving her body in near-flawless consort with the others in the class.

Through spring changes and thoracic twists, Madison's world becomes focused only on the burn in her muscles, the sharpness of her breath, the heightening of her heart rate. She becomes thoroughly sweaty and, when the exercise is concluded forty-five minutes later, Madison feels euphoric, the way she always does after such exercise. It is why she pays the three hundred dollars a month for the privilege of attending these classes.

Madison, like every other person since time unknowable, sacrifices greatly to attain the thing she wants, because it makes her feel good.

After a quick chat with the instructor, Madison leaves the Pilates studio. As she sits in her car, the playlist now on a lower volume as it no longer must fight with the sounds of the highway to be heard, she consults the Tasks app on her phone for the rest of her day's itinerary.

Doing the math in her head, she allots herself fifteen minutes to get coffee, one hour to browse the racks at Target, thirty minutes to stop at the store for the salmon fillets needed for dinner that evening, and then two hours of quiet time before her husband arrives home from work, during which she hopes to complete several assignments of her online degree that are coming close to due. After that, she will need to prepare the house for the arrival of her in-laws, who will be joining them to eat the salmon she's set to purchase.

Madison is satisfied with her busy day. She enjoys having a clear roadmap of her day's events, finding comfort in the structure.

Getting coffee is up first, so Madison drives five minutes down the road and enters her favorite café, a local shop that opened only a few months before. It is important to Madison that, when she can, she supports small businesses and local trade. She only orders things from Amazon if she can't find them easily elsewhere, or if she forgets and needs an item as quickly as possible.

Her coffee is perfect as usual, and she imagines she can taste the love and passion for coffee-making in every sip. She waves goodbye to the barista-slash-owner, wishing him a great day and promising to see him next time.

Then she's onto Target, where she picks out a few pairs of leggings in bright colors. Madison prefers to buy most things in colors if it is an option: she doesn't understand people who can live in a world of neutrals and grays. Her car is an example of this: a bright leaf green.

Purchases bagged, Madison returns to her car, consults Tasks once again, and readjusts her time allotments. She has spent only forty minutes at Target, so she has twenty extra minutes. She decides to use this extra time to make a quick stop at the library. Her intention is to go to the Fiction section and select the book with the brightest-hued spine on the shelf. Madison does not read as much as she would like to; her online courses currently demand too much of her time. But this is a good day, she tells herself, and she wants to spend some time nurturing herself.

The recycled Target bag rustles in the front seat, her new purchases still tagged and neatly folded. Her coffee, now half gone and slightly watered down from the melting ice, sloshes in the cupholder as she drives over a pothole. Madison feels fantastic; she is still euphoric from a great workout, the blood pumping in her body seemingly full of renewed life. Her coffee is still delicious despite the melting ice, and she is already picturing herself in her bright new leggings at tomorrow's Pilates class.

Madison turns down the road on which the library sits, a residential area full of trees and greenery. She is already anticipating the smell of books, that focused, academic scent that always makes her want to sit down at one of the light wood tables and study an anthropology text for hours, feeling her brain and its pathways expanding, her understanding of this world deepening that much more.

Madison's car is traveling twenty-eight miles per hour, as it is a residential area. She doesn't speed in town, only on the highway, and only a little bit. Her Corolla begins to pass through the intersection of Riverside and Poplar, and as it does, a man driving a twenty-year-old Ford pickup at forty miles per hour ignores the stop sign, smashing directly into Madison's side of the Corolla, crushing her body into pulp and severing her spinal column. She dies after only a few confused seconds, and her world, which was previously confined to the interior of her car and the sounds of her playlist and the taste of her coffee and the rustle of the Target bag is now irreplaceably gone.

The Tasks app, still open on her phone, will remain forever unfinished. At the time of her death, she only had fifteen minutes before she needed to be arriving at the store to pick up the salmon. Now, her husband's parents will not come over that evening to eat salmon and catch up and take a look at that electrical socket that only works half the time. Her husband's parents will come over that day to console her husband as he shrieks in a crumpled ball on the couch.

Madison will not wear her new brightly colored leggings to Pilates the next day. The class will happen without her, and the instructor, whom she only knows slightly, will notice Madison's absence but not with grief, only vague curiosity. She will learn that Madison is dead when her husband calls a week later to cancel her membership.

The barista-slash-owner of Madison's favorite café will notice that she no longer comes in on Saturdays, Sundays and Wednesdays, but other things occupy his time and he does not learn of her fate before she fades from his awareness.

Madison is only twenty-four when she dies, and all of her little enjoyments in life, her miniscule but vast worlds that changed with every shift in awareness, are lost forever in a single moment. A single, random moment.

There's a stop sign in my neighborhood that people run quite often. I've nearly been hit three times now, just a street away from my house. Something that I think of often, when I hear of accidents and freak-deaths, is how terrifying I find that concept. Existing one moment, with all of your little quirks and wants and dislikes, gone in the next. Whether this ending bothered you or not, I think this is the scariest story in this collection.

For Jakk

STEPHEN IS OKAY

This is another piece that just kind of came out of nowhere. I started it at work, then went home and finished it in a haze, growling at my husband whenever he tried to speak to me. Not really. Maybe. But it's creepy, it's sad, and it's also about combat trauma.

When Stephen came back from Afghanistan, he expected to feel strange.

He thought the walls of his house would seem too thin, too fragile against barrages of fire and bombs and bullets.

But no fire or bombs or bullets rained down on Stephen's house, so he thought he must be okay.

He thought he would jump at firecrackers on New Year's and the Fourth, primed to think his life was moments from ending, like it had been for five years straight.

But his life did not end with every pop and crack, so he thought he must be okay.

So Stephen went on with his life after he returned home. He had no wife to call him emotionless, no desire for a service dog. He expected to change. To feel strange. He expected what soldiers dread the way sailors dread scurvy: good ol' pal PTSD.

But Stephen was okay.

Until the sand.

When Stephen visited the Oregon coast five years after he came back from Afghanistan, he saw sand for the second time in his life. The first and only other time had been during his deployment.

He'd gotten his degree on the GI Bill dime and landed a job easily in product development. After a particularly great quarter marked by several successful pitches in a row, Stephen was gifted two things: a reserved parking spot, and a paid vacation to the Oregon coast.

Stephen took the trip with neutral enthusiasm. Any excuse to read his books in a chair and drink coffee for a few days in a nice place was welcome, but he'd never had a specific desire to see another beach, another ocean.

Stephen's thoughts turned to his unfulfilled expectations as he drove north on I-5 on his way to Newport, where his free hotel room awaited him.

Five years on and he didn't melt down at the sound of cars backfiring. Five years on and he wasn't plagued by nightmares of the people he'd killed, of the people he'd watched as they died. It surprised Stephen in a mild way, much like the gifting of his coast trip.

Stephen was okay. He concluded that he'd simply gotten lucky.

He spent his first night on the Oregon coast relaxing in his hotel room, his battered paperback barely leaving his hands. He drank all the free coffee provided to his room by the hotel staff, then called down to ask for more.

He spent his first full day on the Oregon coast relaxing in his hotel room until 6 o'clock, when he realized something. He should at least go out and see the ocean. Maybe he could read his book out there, listen to the waves, breathe the damp salty air.

Subsequently, Stephen was stretched out in the sand, book in his hand, toes in the ocean, when he saw the sand move beside him.

He thought of a movie he'd seen as a child: *Labyrinth*. The way the practical effects had made a bog bubble up so realistically, the way the filthy brownish water had risen and fallen like the filling lungs of some shapeless monster right beneath the surface.

The way the sand beside him moved was like the rise and fall of a chest with the intake of air, very much like that bog. Stephen had read about crabs that burrowed under beach sand, about how sea turtles hatch beneath the sand before making their life-or-death run to the ocean. He jumped to his feet, clutching his book in a death grip, and took several steps away. His hand reached out and snatched his recently purchased Dollar Tree towel from the sand, then watched.

The sand continued to rise and fall, slowly, like the beach itself was breathing. The space was not very large, maybe a foot at its widest, and slightly ovular.

As Stephen watched it rise and fall, he found there was something tickling the back of his mind, the way he felt when he knew he'd forgotten something in the morning but couldn't remember what. Something nagging, insistent, barely tangible.

He stared at the spot of breathing sand and felt his hands open, felt them drop his book and his towel. His eyes drifted downward to find his feet moving, bringing him back toward the moving spot.

I have to… Have to get it out, he thought nonsensically, and then the thought was gone, replaced by action.

Stephen knelt before the rising sand and reached his hands down, slowly scooping up handfuls of moist sand, dropping them to the sides.

He knew what he was doing in a vague way that was outside of himself: thought *I am digging in the sand*, but could not think more critically about his actions than that. He could not stop, did not wonder why he was doing it, just kept digging with nothing but his hands and nails.

The skin of his hands turned red and raw, and his right index finger stung with a slice from a sharp rock that had been embedded in the sand. Finally, he stopped digging. He was finished, but he didn't understand why.

Until he blinked, clearing his mind, and looked down at the hole.

Buried several inches deep in the wet sand was a face.

The skin was brown, darker than the sand around it. The mouth was open in a scream, displaying the chipped and crooked teeth signature to third world countries, where dentistry was a privilege. The eyes, whites popping out, bulged from the face in terror, matching the silent scream of the mouth. The face was small and thin, and it took Stephen a long, paralyzed moment to under-stand that he was looking at the awkward face of a young teenager.

Then the eyes moved, locked gazes with Stephen.

Stephen cried out and tumbled over, wetting his back with damp sand and seeing black spots as his head slammed to the ground.

He knew the face.

As his vision darkened momentarily from the impact of his fall, he saw the face looking at him again, not from its place buried in the sand, but as Stephen had last seen it, nearly six years ago now. A boy, barely a teenager, automatic rifle slung over his shoulder that looked so big and heavy on his lean frame that he should be leaning to one side. The look of surprise and barely-processed fear turning to a scream as he saw Stephen's arm extend, throwing the active grenade directly at him.

Stephen groaned as he pulled himself up to a seated position in the sand. *It was a dream, a break in reality, just a hallucination.* These thoughts comforted him until he lifted his head and peered out at the sand where the face had just been.

It was no longer there. Instead, a thin brown arm reached up and out of the hole Stephen had dug. It slapped against the sand and the muscles flexed as it pulled itself up. Then came the boy's head, shoulders, and torso, bare and gritty with beach sand that clung to the skin.

The boy stared at Stephen the entire time as he pulled himself slowly from inside the beach. His eyes, still frozen in surprise and fear, did not blink or move. The mouth, frozen in the silent scream, gaped at Stephen like a dark cave.

When the boy began to lift one leg out of the hole, Stephen's paralysis broke.

He turned and ran, grunting in choppy heaves as he flew with utter terror, the most he had ever felt, even during his deployment.

Behind him, he could hear the damp slap of bare feet against wet sand.

A whimper escaped him, and tears of fear stung his eyes as he flew past carefree beachgoers, propped up on their elbows on blankets to marvel at his terrified flight.

When his lungs began to burn and he felt bile rising in his throat, Stephen slowed and forced himself to look back.

The boy was gone.

There was only one set of footprints behind him, trailing all the way back to where he could barely see the speck on the sand that was his towel and book.

It wasn't real, it's okay, it wasn't real, he repeated over and over to himself, huffing and heaving as he worked to suck air into his burning lungs. *It was only a hallucination. It wasn't really there. It was about time I started cracking a bit anyways, right? I was bound to crack. It was going to happen sooner or later.*

His thoughts continued to race as he stood there on the beach, giving an embarrassed wave to the woman and her two kids still staring at him. He knew he'd looked insane, running at top speed from nothing.

"Wasp," he called out to them as an explanation.

They nodded and went back to their play and conversation at this, and Stephen found that his breath was mostly back to normal.

Just a hallucination, he thought again. *It wasn't real so it can't hurt you.*

I'm okay.

By the time Stephen returned to his hotel room, he was feeling ten kinds of foolish. That boy was dead, long dead. Stephen had seen his arms land on different sides of the road. He couldn't be here, now, following Stephen after nearly six years.

Stephen chuckled with nervous relief as he tapped his key card against his door lock. It beeped and the little light turned green, and Stephen pushed the door open, breathing in the clean linen scent of his hotel room.

He set his key card and wallet down on the desk, then bent over and removed his shoes. They were, of course, full of sand. He had been expecting to have sand everywhere after his beach escapade, especially after the way he'd fallen backward. It was in his shorts, inside his shirt.

Stephen threw the door's deadbolt behind him and began peeling off his damp, sandy clothes. He turned and entered the bathroom, eager for a shower, for the feeling of smooth, clean skin. Showers always did wonders to refresh his mind. He knew he would feel ten times better about his little psychotic slip after he'd spent some time in the steamy water.

Stephen pulled open the shower curtain and froze.

Inside the bathtub was several inches of sand. It covered the entire length of the tub, and it was bumpy on the surface, like the beach had been bumpy from the passing feet of endless beachgoers.

What— Stephen thought, stumbling backward. He felt his lower back hit the sink behind him.

Then the sound started, coming from outside the bathroom.

Wet footsteps, those of bare feet slapping against damp sand.

For Mr. Klug

OUR HAPPINESS

This final story is not scary. It is quite the opposite. Inspired by the prompt for Fractured Lit's 2025 Elsewhere Prize, I wrote it without hardly taking a breath. The prompt was to make the ordinary extraordinary, or vice versa. I like to think I did both. It's my shortest piece, but it expresses the way I view happiness and how simple it can really be. I hope you're reading it in your favorite chair with a cup of coffee in your hand, just the way you like it.

I find the alien in the woods by my cottage.

His little silver craft smokes. At first, I worry he is dead. Under the smell of the ancient pines, I can smell burning flesh.

I pull him carefully from the dented metal and smoldering splinters of broken branches. He respires shakily, but I worry he will not last long.

His small form is limp and feverish as I carry him back to my small home. He stirs but does not make any sound.

I carry him inside. He weighs less than five pounds, by my estimate. Much more, and my old bones would crack under the strain.

I sit beside him. He's laid out on my sofa, a quilt I made draped over his strange body. When he wakes, I am surprised but not afraid. He is too small, too injured to be a danger to me, old and frail as I am.

His eyes open. There are eight, and they are completely black as a night unbroken by city lights.

No distinguishing marks or appendages mark him as male to me, but he possesses nothing like hair or breasts, so I call him "he" in my head. It is for my benefit only.

Those inky black eyes, eight by count, look at my cottage, the quilt, the sofa. I don't know how I know this, with no discernible pupils to see, but I do. His eyes shift in some way that is hard to understand.

Then he speaks.

The sound is foreign. A new type of sound. It does not sound like anything I've heard before, because it is not a sound of this place. It is like discovering a new color.

"I'm sorry, I don't understand," I tell him, knowing he will not understand me either, but needing to say something. "I hope you're alright. You're burned quite badly," I ramble, trying to fill the silence that never seemed this large when it was just me in this house. "I have some gauze and ointment, assuming they will work on you." I give a light, nervous laugh. This is mad. An alien has crash landed outside my cottage in the middle of nowhere, and I'm offering it Neosporin.

"I do not require medicine, female," comes an odd, warping voice. He has nothing I can identify as a mouth, but it could only be him.

"You understand me?" I gasp.

"I have translation abilities, female," he responds. "And I will heal shortly by natural process."

"You can call me Beth," I say, fighting down more giggles at the absurdity of the situation.

"I am now healed, Beth," he says.

"That fast?" I say, amazed.

"Yes. Kindly show me your happiness, Beth."

This makes me stop short. I wonder if his 'translation abilities' are imperfect. "You mean this?" I ask, and give him a large, exaggerated smile.

He moves quickly from his position on the couch, coming to stand before me before I understand it's happened. Everything is fast with this creature.

I am not afraid, still. I am old and satisfied, and death is a next-door neighbor now.

"No, Beth. Kindly show me your happiness."

"I don't understand what you mean," I say, my comical smile turning sheepish. He is inches away. Apparently it is an acceptable distance wherever he comes from.

"I am here to see your happiness. The thing that creates that, Beth," he says, and points a ten-fingered clawlike hand at my unsure smile.

Understanding dawns on me. "Oh," I say, and laugh. "What makes me happy!"

"Yes, Beth."

I think about it for only a moment. I know myself very well at this age.

"I like waking up in the morning and-"

"Stop, Beth," he interrupts, and my mouth snaps shut. "Kindly show me your happiness."

This stops me again. I consider.

"Alright," I say, and get to my feet. "But it's too late for those things right now. You'll have to stay here until the morning to see my exciting life firsthand," I joke. His face remains unchanged. If he has eyelids, he has not used them to blink yet.

"I will stay, Beth."

"Do you need anything before I go to sleep? Another blanket, something to… eat?"

"No, Beth. I will wait for you to sleep, then you will show me your happiness."

When I wake, I expect him to be gone. Either he never existed at all, or he tired of waiting for me to rise.

He is still there. Still standing in the exact spot, the exact position I left him in. But I can feel the eight void-like eyes turn to me. I still don't know how I know.

"Alright. Here's what makes me happy," I announce with amusement.

He moves very quickly again, almost impossible for me to see. He is beside me. I don't mind or move away.

I grind my coffee beans by hand, then brew it and add some milk bought from the farm some ten miles away, my nearest neighbor. The rich, earthy smell fills my cottage, and I breathe it in and smile.

"This is happiness," he says. For the first time there is something like emotion in his voice.

"Wait for the best part," I say, and walk past him and out the front door. He follows soundlessly.

My rocking chair has beads of morning dew on its worn cushion. I sit on them, uncaring, and inhale the scent of the pines, of a new day in nature, of fresh born sunshine.

And I sip my coffee, beginning to rock lightly.

"This is happiness," I sigh, and smile at my unexpected visitor.

He stands there and watches me, unmoving, until my cup is almost empty.

"Thank you for sharing your happiness with me, Beth," he says. "Now it is our happiness."

For you, reader. Thank you.

ACKNOWLEDGMENTS

There are a lot of people who were integral to the writing of these stories. I'll do my best to be quick!

My parents, for always supporting whatever thing it is that I want to do- whether it's singing in a punk band, learning to play violin (abandoned quickly), or writing fiction, they have never once discouraged me in any endeavor. Y'all, this is a rare thing and I do not take you guys for granted. Thank you.

My husband Jesse, who always ensures I have whatever I need to get things done. Jesse, you've always believed in me with this strange certainty. Never knew where it came from.

My writing partner L. Saige Johnson (Saige to me), who has given me unwavering support since the beginning of my writing journey. Saige, my writing would not be what it is without you. Thanks for all the "can I send you this chapter so you can tell me if it's awful or not", every "just got another rejection!", and each "manifest for me". Starting Pen & Sword with you has been great for my productivity and my relationship with my own writing. Here's to a million more blog posts!

My brother Michael, for ferrying my rough drafts home for my dad to read. A thankless job.

My first real reader, Clara, who read my *Saw*-style shock horror flash in middle school and made me understand for the first time that my words actually can make people feel things. Thanks for always being one out of three people to like my Instagram posts!

My cousin Walt, who is an actual real author (see *100 Depictions of Zach Galifianakis*, 2010). Walt, your beta read feedback has only ever been incredibly helpful, and your work has always been an inspiration to me. Shameless plug—check out Walt's work at www.waltcarlson.net.

My artiste en résidence, Olivia, who has drawn so much beautiful character art for me at this point, we may as well just call her my Artistic Director. Olivia, you've only ever been enthusiastic about bringing my characters and concepts to life, and having your depictions on hand has only helped to solidify my sense of each character. I couldn't have asked for a more fitting cover piece than this one. Here's to many more!

Every one of the Six Guys- Saige, Olivia, Nick, Cody, and Jesse- you've been there for all my moments of despair, rage, hopelessness, and triumph. Thank you for your endless patience with my rants.

My bosses, Jason and Brandon. I know you know I wrote most of this stuff while on the clock. Thanks for letting me be me.

My new friends at *Tumbleweird*- Sara Quinn, editor in chief, and Lari, world's best copyeditor. You guys put me in print for the very first time, and continue to champion every story I send your way. Keep it weird!

My dad, again, for being my beta reader for everything. The manuscripts for almost all of these stories were in my dad's hands the moment they were first finished, and his contributions and edits have been absolutely invaluable. I'm so thankful that we can share in our love of the written word. Hopefully someday, when I'm all famous and stuff, the guys at Tor will let me use you as an editor.

Finally, to you. Because whoever you are, you are holding my collection in your hands right now, and in order to do that, you would've had to support me in some way. That's absolutely invaluable. I can scream into the void and punch my computer when I try to format page numbers all I want, but none of it means anything without you. Thank you.

Pasco, Washington
December 21st, 2025

ABOUT THE AUTHOR

Photo by Angela Garcia-Moog

AVA CHRISTINA is a writer of fantasy and horror stories, often blurring the lines between the two. Her short fiction has been published in *Dark Harbor, The Bleeding Margin* and *Tumbleweird.* Her biggest influence is Stephen King, whom she considers to be the master of charact-erization. She currently has a handful of novel projects scattered across several genres, including fantasy, horror, romance, sci-fi, and western. She lives in eastern Washington with her husband and four cats.

www.penandsword.blog
Instagram: @ac_bookaddict

www.ingramcontent.com/pod-product-compliance
Lightning Source LLC
LaVergne TN
LVHW090514110826
845146LV00003B/857

* 9 7 9 8 2 1 8 9 1 2 8 4 0 *